THE PELICAN SHAKESPEARE

GENERAL EDITOR ALFRED HARBAGE

MACBETH

WILLIAM SHAKESPEARE

MACBETH

EDITED BY ALFRED HARBAGE

PENGUIN BOOKS

PENGUIN BOOKS
Published by the Penguin Group
Viking Penguin Inc., 40 West 23rd Street,
New York, New York 10010, U.S.A.
Penguin Books Ltd, 27 Wrights Lane,
London W8 5TZ, England
Penguin Books Australia Ltd, Ringwood,
Victoria, Australia
Penguin Books Canada Ltd, 2801 John Street,
Markham, Ontario, Canada L3R 1B4
Penguin Books (N.Z.) Ltd, 182–190 Wairau Road,
Auckland 10, New Zealand

Penguin Books Ltd, Registered Offices:
Harmondsworth, Middlesex, England

First published in *The Pelican Shakespeare* 1956
This revised edition first published 1971

21   23   25   24   22

Copyright © Penguin Books, Inc., 1956, 1971
Copyright renewed Viking Penguin Inc., 1984
All rights reserved

Library of Congress catalog card number: 79-98373
ISBN 0 14 0714.01 4

Printed in the United States of America
Set in Monotype Ehrhardt

CONTENTS

PUBLISHER'S NOTE

Soon after the thirty-eight volumes forming *The Pelican Shake-speare* had been published, they were brought together in *The Complete Pelican Shakespeare*. The editorial revisions and new textual features are explained in detail in the General Editor's Preface to the one-volume edition. They have all been incorporated in the present volume. The following should be mentioned in particular:

The lines are not numbered in arbitrary units. Instead all lines are numbered which contain a word, phrase, or allusion explained in the glossarial notes. In the occasional instances where there is a long stretch of unannotated text, certain lines are numbered in italics to serve the conventional reference purpose.

The intrusive and often inaccurate place-headings inserted by early editors are omitted (as is becoming standard practise), but for the convenience of those who miss them, an indication of locale now appears as first item in the annotation of each scene.

In the interest of both elegance and utility, each speech-prefix is set in a separate line when the speaker's lines are in verse, except when these words form the second half of a pentameter line. Thus the verse form of the speech is kept visually intact, and turned-over lines are avoided. What is printed as verse and what is printed as prose has, in general, the authority of the original texts. Departures from the original texts in this regard have only the authority of editorial tradition and the judgment of the Pelican editors; and, in a few instances, are admittedly arbitrary.

SHAKESPEARE AND
HIS STAGE

William Shakespeare was christened in Holy Trinity Church, Stratford-upon-Avon, April 26, 1564. His birth is traditionally assigned to April 23. He was the eldest of four boys and two girls who survived infancy in the family of John Shakespeare, glover and trader of Henley Street, and his wife Mary Arden, daughter of a small landowner of Wilmcote. In 1568 John was elected Bailiff (equivalent to Mayor) of Stratford, having already filled the minor municipal offices. The town maintained for the sons of the burgesses a free school, taught by a university graduate and offering preparation in Latin sufficient for university entrance; its early registers are lost, but there can be little doubt that Shakespeare received the formal part of his education in this school.

On November 27, 1582, a license was issued for the marriage of William Shakespeare (aged eighteen) and Ann Hathaway (aged twenty-six), and on May 26, 1583, their child Susanna was christened in Holy Trinity Church. The inference that the marriage was forced upon the youth is natural but not inevitable; betrothal was legally binding at the time, and was sometimes regarded as conferring conjugal rights. Two additional children of the marriage, the twins Hamnet and Judith, were christened on February 2, 1585. Meanwhile the prosperity of the elder Shakespeares had declined, and William was impelled to seek a career outside Stratford.

The tradition that he spent some time as a country

teacher is old but unverifiable. Because of the absence of records his early twenties are called the "lost years," and only one thing about them is certain – that at least some of these years were spent in winning a place in the acting profession. He may have begun as a provincial trouper, but by 1592 he was established in London and prominent enough to be attacked. In a pamphlet of that year, *Groats-worth of Wit*, the ailing Robert Greene complained of the neglect which university writers like himself had suffered from actors, one of whom was daring to set up as a playwright :

. . . an vpstart Crow, beautified with our feathers, that with his *Tygers hart wrapt in a Players hyde*, supposes he is as well able to bombast out a blanke verse as the best of you: and beeing an absolute *Iohannes fac totum*, is in his owne conceit the onely Shake-scene in a countrey.

The pun on his name, and the parody of his line "O tiger's heart wrapped in a woman's hide" (*3 Henry VI*), pointed clearly to Shakespeare. Some of his admirers protested, and Henry Chettle, the editor of Greene's pamphlet, saw fit to apologize :

. . . I am as sory as if the originall fault had beene my fault, because my selfe haue seene his demeanor no lesse ciuill than he excelent in the qualitie he professes : Besides, diuers of worship haue reported his vprightnes of dealing, which argues his honesty, and his facetious grace in writting, that approoues his Art. (Prefatory epistle, *Kind-Harts Dreame*)

The plague closed the London theatres for many months in 1592–94, denying the actors their livelihood. To this period belong Shakespeare's two narrative poems, *Venus and Adonis* and *The Rape of Lucrece*, both dedicated to the Earl of Southampton. No doubt the poet was rewarded with a gift of money as usual in such cases, but he did no further dedicating and we have no reliable information on whether Southampton, or anyone else, became his regular patron. His sonnets, first mentioned in 1598 and published without his consent in 1609, are intimate without being explicitly autobiographical. They seem to commemorate the poet's friendship with an idealized youth, rivalry with a more favored poet, and love affair with a dark mistress; and his bitterness when the mistress betrays him in conjunction with the friend; but it is difficult to decide precisely what the "story" is, impossible to decide whether it is fictional or true. The true distinction of the sonnets, at least of those not purely conventional, rests in the universality of the thoughts and moods they express, and in their poignancy and beauty.

In 1594 was formed the theatrical company known until 1603 as the Lord Chamberlain's men, thereafter as the King's men. Its original membership included, besides Shakespeare, the beloved clown Will Kempe and the famous actor Richard Burbage. The company acted in various London theatres and even toured the provinces, but it is chiefly associated in our minds with the Globe Theatre built on the south bank of the Thames in 1599. Shakespeare was an actor and joint owner of this company (and its Globe) through the remainder of his creative years. His plays, written at the average rate of two a year, together with Burbage's acting won it its place of leadership among the London companies.

Individual plays began to appear in print, in editions both honest and piratical, and the publishers became increasingly aware of the value of Shakespeare's name on the title pages. As early as 1598 he was hailed as the leading English dramatist in the *Palladis Tamia* of Francis Meres:

As *Plautus* and *Seneca* are accounted the best for Comedy and Tragedy among the Latines, so *Shakespeare* among the English is the most excellent in both kinds for the stage: for Comedy, witnes his *Gentlemen of Verona*, his *Errors*, his *Loue labors lost*, his *Loue labours wonne* [at one time in print but no longer extant, at least under this title], his *Midsummers night dream*, & his *Merchant of Venice*; for Tragedy, his *Richard the 2*, *Richard the 3*, *Henry the 4*, *King Iohn*, *Titus Andronicus*, and his *Romeo and Iuliet*.

The note is valuable both in indicating Shakespeare's prestige and in helping us to establish a chronology. In the second half of his writing career, history plays gave place to the great tragedies; and farces and light comedies gave place to the problem plays and symbolic romances. In 1623, seven years after his death, his former fellow-actors, John Heminge and Henry Condell, cooperated with a group of London printers in bringing out his plays in collected form. The volume is generally known as the First Folio.

Shakespeare had never severed his relations with Stratford. His wife and children may sometimes have shared his London lodgings, but their home was Stratford. His son Hamnet was buried there in 1596, and his daughters Susanna and Judith were married there in 1607 and 1616 respectively. (His father, for whom he had secured a coat of arms and thus the privilege of writing himself gentleman, died in 1601, his mother in 1608.) His considerable earnings in London, as actor-sharer, part owner of the Globe, and playwright, were invested chiefly in Stratford property. In 1597 he purchased for £60 New Place, one of the two most imposing residences in the town. A number of other business transactions, as well as minor episodes in his career, have left documentary records. By 1611 he was in a position to retire, and he seems gradually to have withdrawn from theatrical activity in order to live in Stratford. In March, 1616, he made a will, leaving token bequests to Burbage, Heminge, and Condell, but the bulk of his estate to his family. The most famous feature of the will, the bequest of the second-best bed to his wife, reveals nothing about Shakespeare's marriage; the quaintness of the provision seems commonplace to those familiar with ancient testaments. Shakespeare died April 23, 1616, and was buried in the Stratford church where he had been christened. Within seven years a monument was erected to his memory on the north wall of the chancel. Its portrait bust and the Droeshout engraving on the title page of the First Folio provide the only likenesses with an established claim to authenticity. The best verbal vignette was written by his rival Ben Jonson, the more impressive for being imbedded in a context mainly critical:

. . . I loved the man, and doe honour his memory (on this side idolatry) as much as any. Hee was indeed honest, and of an open and free nature: had an excellent Phantsie, brave notions, and gentle expressions. . . . (*Timber or Discoveries*, ca. 1623-30)

*

The reader of Shakespeare's plays is aided by a general knowledge of the way in which they were staged. The King's men acquired a roofed and artificially lighted theatre only toward the close of Shakespeare's career, and then only for winter use. Nearly all his plays were designed for performance in such structures as the Globe – a three-tiered amphitheatre with a large rectangular platform extending to the center of its yard. The plays were staged by daylight, by large casts brilliantly costumed, but with only a minimum of properties, without scenery, and quite possibly without intermissions. There was a rear stage gallery for action "above," and a curtained rear recess for "discoveries" and other special effects, but by far the major portion of any play was enacted upon the projecting platform, with episode following episode in swift succession, and with shifts of time and place signaled the audience only by the momentary clearing of the stage between the episodes. Information about the identity of the characters and, when necessary, about the time and place of the action was incorporated in the dialogue. No place-headings have been inserted in the present editions; these are apt to obscure the original fluidity of structure, with the emphasis upon action and speech rather than scenic background. (Indications of place are supplied in the footnotes.) The acting, including that of the youthful apprentices to the profession who performed the parts of women, was highly skillful, with a premium placed upon grace of gesture and beauty of diction. The audiences, a cross section of the general public, commonly numbered a thousand, sometimes more than two thousand. Judged by the type of plays they applauded, these audiences were not only large but also perceptive.

THE TEXTS OF THE PLAYS

About half of Shakespeare's plays appeared in print for the first time in the folio volume of 1623. The others had been published individually, usually in quarto volumes, during his lifetime or in the six years following his death. The copy used by the printers of the quartos varied greatly in merit, sometimes representing Shakespeare's true text, sometimes only a debased version of that text. The copy used by the printers of the folio also varied in merit, but was chosen with care. Since it consisted of the best available manuscripts, or the more acceptable quartos (although frequently in editions other than the first), or of quartos corrected by reference to manuscripts, we have good or reasonably good texts of most of the thirty-seven plays.

In the present series, the plays have been newly edited from quarto or folio texts, depending, when a choice offered, upon which is now regarded by bibliographical specialists as the more authoritative. The ideal has been to reproduce the chosen texts with as few alterations as possible, beyond occasional relineation, expansion of abbreviations, and modernization of punctuation and spelling. Emendation is held to a minimum, and such material as has been added, in the way of stage directions and lines supplied by an alternative text, has been enclosed in square brackets.

None of the plays printed in Shakespeare's lifetime were divided into acts and scenes, and the inference is that the author's own manuscripts were not so divided. In the folio collection, some of the plays remained undivided, some were divided into acts, and some were divided into acts and scenes. During the eighteenth century all of the plays were divided into acts and scenes, and in the Cambridge edition of the mid-nineteenth century, from which the influential Globe text derived, this division was more or less regularized and the lines were numbered. Many useful works of reference employ the act–scene–line apparatus thus established.

Since this act–scene division is obviously convenient, but is of very dubious authority so far as Shakespeare's own structural principles are concerned, or the original manner of staging his plays, a problem is presented to modern editors. In the present series the act–scene division is retained marginally, and may be viewed as a reference aid like the line numbering. A star marks the points of division when these points have been determined by a cleared stage indicating a shift of time and place in the action of the play, or when no harm results from the editorial assumption that there is such a shift. However, at those points where the established division is clearly misleading – that is, where continuous action has been split up into separate "scenes" – the star is omitted and the distortion corrected. This mechanical expedient seemed the best means of combining utility and accuracy.

THE GENERAL EDITOR

INTRODUCTION

Macbeth is the shortest of Shakespeare's tragedies and the simplest in its statement: *Thou shalt not kill*. In the words of Coleridge, it contains "no reasonings of equivocal morality, . . . no sophistry of self-delusion." With eyes wide open to the hideousness of his offense, a brave, imaginative, and morally sensitive man commits a stealthy murder for gain. His victim is his guest, his benefactor, his kinsman, and his king; and to shield himself from detection he incontinently sacrifices the lives and reputation of two innocent underlings. The retribution is as appalling as the crime – his soul's slow death in self-horror, degradation, loneliness, and despair, then his bloody extermination.

Why should such a man do such evil? That we ask the question instead of dismissing the play as an incredible fiction is our tribute to the poet's vision and artistry. The question reshapes itself on our lips, Why is there evil for men to do? and we realize that there can be no answer. The core of *Macbeth* is a religious mystery, its moral clarity a testament of faith. Evil may be recognized, loathed, and combated without being understood: " . . . in these cases / We still have judgment here."

The earliest mention of the play occurs in notes on a performance at the Globe, April 20, 1611, by the spectator Simon Forman, but the style and a few shreds of literary evidence suggest 1605–06 as the period of composition; hence it followed *Hamlet*, *Othello*, and possibly also *Lear*, those other tragedies in which destruction is wrought by naked evil, not mere domestic or political strife. *Macbeth* differs from the other three in that the evil works through the protagonist as well as upon him. The one with whom we identify is the one who is possessed; this citadel crumbles from within. The supernatural soliciting of the Weird Sisters, the strenuous persuasions of the wife, do not explain Macbeth's guilt. They enhance its power over our imagination by revealing stages in its course and suggesting forces in perilous balance.

In Holinshed's *Chronicle*, from which Shakespeare drew his material, adding to the sins of the semi-legendary Macbeth those of Donwald, slayer of King Duff, the Weird Sisters are "goddesses of destinie" derived from a heathen fatalism. In the play they are Elizabethan witches, their prescriptive powers subtly curtailed; they predict, abet, and symbolize damnation but do not determine it. Any sense that Macbeth is a helpless victim, his crime predestined, his will bound, is canceled as the play proceeds. We may seem to see in the encounter on the heath the very inception of his lethal designs, but we should ask with Banquo,

> Good sir, why do you start and seem to fear
> Things that do sound so fair?

Nothing in the witches' prophecies would have suggested to an untainted mind that to "be King hereafter" meant to be murderer first. That Macbeth was already tainted would have been apparent to the original audience. In another play of the era, *The Witch of Edmonton*, the black dog appears at her side only when the wish for his presence is wrung from old Mother Sawyer's lips. The stars could influence but could not govern, the devils could come but only upon summons. At some unknown time for some unknown reason Macbeth has corrupted in pride, and has contemplated the sale of his soul as certainly as Faustus. When we later discover through the words of his Lady that plans to murder Duncan had preceded the meeting on the heath, we should not bring charges of inconsistency, speculate about "lost scenes," or complain that we have been tricked.

The prophecies, nevertheless, without explaining or excusing Macbeth's crimes, impress us as mitigation: powerful and wily forces are speeding him on his course. The more earthly influence of his Lady's persuasions impresses us in a similar way. They provide, moreover, an occasion for the display of his aversion for what he is about to do, and convert it, at least in some measure, from utter self-serving into an offering to her. Lady Macbeth's own behavior is not totally alienating. In a perverted way she is doing what all loyal wives are expected to do, urging her husband on to what she deems his good; here, as in the period of danger that follows, she at least is *all for him*. This is one of the marvels of the play, the manner in which this frightful collusion proceeds in an atmosphere of domestic virtue without the effect of irony. If the evil is great it is also limited, even in respect to the malefactors. After the Lady's collapse, her initial ferocity is remembered as something false to her nature, and the solicitude of her wise and kindly physician seems to us not misplaced.

Macbeth himself is as humane in his reflections as he is inhuman in his acts. Like Iago he is a moralizing villain, but his moralizing is not clever aphoristic display. It comes from his heart, sometimes like an echo of ancient folk beliefs,

> It will have blood, they say : blood will have blood.
> Stones have been known to move and trees to speak ;
> Augures and understood relations have
> By maggot-pies and choughs and rooks brought forth
> The secret'st man of blood –

sometimes like religious revelation,

> [Duncan's] virtues
> Will plead like angels, trumpet-tongued against

> The deep damnation of his taking-off;
> And pity, like a naked new-born babe
> Striding the blast, or heaven's cherubin horsed
> Upon the sightless couriers of the air,
> Shall blow the horrid deed in every eye
> That tears shall drown the wind.

No voice in literature has sounded with greater sadness :

> I have lived long enough. My way of life
> Is fall'n into the sear, the yellow leaf,
> And that which should accompany old age,
> As honor, love, obedience, troops of friends,
> I must not look to have ; but, in their stead,
> Curses not loud but deep, mouth-honor, breath,
> Which the poor heart would fain deny, and dare not.

To say that no one who has become a bloody tyrant would speak in this way is pointless ; he would *feel* in this way, or so we are convinced.

By feeling the pangs that we would feel if we were in his place, and by passing our judgments upon himself, Macbeth attaches us to him and consequently himself to us. We cannot view him with cold objectivity as something strange and apart. The unnaturalness of his acts is always counterpoised by the naturalness of his actions : his hesitant overtures to Banquo, his volubility after Duncan's death, his dazed petulance at the appearance of the ghost,

> The time has been
> That, when the brains were out, the man would die,
> And there an end. But now they rise again,
> With twenty mortal murders on their crowns,
> And push us from our stools.

There is something here both grimly humorous and affecting, this killer's speaking in the accents of a hurt child. We should not ascribe Macbeth's humanity to the automatic working of Shakespeare's sympathetic nature. There is nothing casual about it. If Macbeth were other than he is, less like ourselves, he would be a less powerful symbol of our own worst potentialities and the abyss we have escaped. There is nothing of him in Edmund or Iago for all of Shakespeare's sympathetic nature.

It is hard to believe that so universal a work was calculated to the meridian of any particular person, but there are arguments favoring the possibility. James Stuart, who had ascended the English throne and become the nominal patron of Shakespeare's company a few years before *Macbeth* was written, was supposedly descended from Banquo and was intensely interested in witchcraft; moreover he had assumed in 1605 the prerogative of curing the "king's evil" instituted by Edward the Confessor and mentioned somewhat irrelevantly in the play. On the other hand, one may argue that, had Shakespeare's primary concern been to please the monarch, he might have dramatized more creditable episodes in Scottish history, might have drawn a more flattering portrait of Banquo, and might have seized the opportunity to eulogize James as first holder of the "treble sceptres" mentioned in the show of kings (IV, i). Possibly Shakespeare was responding in his own way to the urgings of his dramatic company; he was in some respects the most reticent writer of his times, and his allusions even to Elizabeth had been few and restrained.

Whether or not *Macbeth* may be considered in a sense "topical" it contains elements that are, or might have been, mere theatrical entertainment. It combines with its great theme the working out of a puzzle, and affords us the pleasure of watching pieces dropping into place. That Macbeth would be king but no father of kings, that he would reign until Birnam Wood marched to Dunsinane, that he would be unconquerable by any man born of woman were riddling prophecies included in Holinshed, but the manner of presenting them through apparitions was Shakespeare's invention: the "Armed Head" instigating the aggression against Macduff probably represents Macbeth himself; the "Child Crowned, with a tree in his hand" certainly represents young Malcolm, deviser of the tactics at Birnam Wood; the "Bloody Child" represents Macduff, who was "from his mother's womb / Untimely ripped." These ingenuities might well have been intrusive in a play so elemental; as handled by Shakespeare they contribute to the master plan by allowing us to watch Macbeth gradually stripped of hope by those "juggling fiends" upon whom he has relied.

The opportunities for spectacularity offered by the play were seized early, and alterations had already been made in the single version that has come down to us, that printed in the folio of 1623. The Hecate scenes (III, v; IV, i, 39–43, 125–32) are interpolations obviously designed in order to introduce songs and dances by the witches. The first words of the songs, "Come away" and "Black spirits," permit us to identify them as having been borrowed from Thomas Middleton's *The Witch*, where their texts appear in full. Who wrote the surrounding matter we do not know, but its quality serves one useful purpose. Such lines as

> O, well done! I commend your pains,
> And every one shall share i' th' gains.
> And now about the cauldron sing
> Like elves and fairies in a ring

make us appreciate the more the magical raucousness of the language that Shakespeare himself gave his witches. The authenticity of the Porter's speech was questioned by Coleridge in one of his critical lapses; this too served a useful purpose, in evoking from De Quincey a gem of literary appreciation. At the Restoration the tradition of spectacular amplification was in full bloom, and on January 7, 1667, Samuel Pepys pronounced a revival as especially excellent "in *divertissement*, though it be a deep tragedy, which is a strange perfection in a tragedy." This "strange perfection" afflicts us still; no other Shakespearean play has provoked more recklessness in the invention of "effects."

Whatever intrudes upon the stark simplicity of this work of art is an offense. It needs no help. Its brevity makes us wonder if there have been cuts as well as additions in the text printed in the folio, but it is hard to imagine any extension that would not have marred its present compact structure. The physical and spiritual terror rises in swift crescendos until Macduff's child is slaughtered at Fife and the universe seems riven in two; then comes the resting place of the scene in England like the still moment at the core of a hurricane; when the blast resumes, it is not to compound chaos but to orchestrate the restoration of moral order. No one who has read the play will ever forget the hardy characters who struggle to readmit light into their murky world, and certainly not that incandescent couple who kill together and die apart. The style has the vigor, condensation, and imaginative splendor of Shakespeare at his greatest, when he seems to be pressing upon the very bounds of the expressible. Blood and darkness are constantly invoked, and jarring antitheses, violent hyperbole, and chaotic imagery give the lines the quality demanded by the action. But there are also moments of unforgettable hush. Some of the speeches seem to express the agony of all mankind :

> Canst thou not minister to a mind diseased,
> Pluck from the memory a rooted sorrow,
> Raze out the written troubles of the brain,
> And with some sweet oblivious antidote
> Cleanse the stuffed bosom of that perilous stuff
> Which weighs upon the heart ?

Over the centuries comes the quiet answer, convincing us, as so often the words of this poet so strangely do, that nothing further can be said,

> Therein the patient
> Must minister to himself.

Harvard University   ALFRED HARBAGE

NOTE ON THE TEXT

The present edition follows closely the only substantive text (folio, 1623), which is mechanically defective but not corrupt in the sense of misrepresenting, in general, Shakespeare's language. The copy was evidently provided by a transcript of a prompt-book. The act–scene division here supplied marginally coincides with the division of the folio text except that V, vii of the latter is subdivided into vii and viii. A more rational point of subdivision comes later (at V, viii, 35) and is marked by some modern editors as scene ix. A stage direction in the folio text indicates that Macbeth was slain in sight of the audience, and this direction is retained in the present text. The body could have been carried offstage by Macduff or another. Except for extensive relineation, the following list of emendations indicates the only material departures from the folio text. The adopted reading in italics is followed by the folio reading in roman.

I, i, 1 *again* again? 9–11 2. *Witch . . . air* (in the folio these lines form a single speech attributed to "All")

I, ii, 13 *gallowglasses* Gallowgrosses 14 *quarrel* Quarry 26 *thunders break* Thunders 56 *point rebellious, arm* point, rebellious arm

I, iii, 32 *weird* weyward 39 *Forres* Soris 98 *Came* Can 109 *borrowed* borrowèd

I, iv, 1 *Are* Or

I, v, 7 *weird* weyward

I, vi, 4 *martlet* Barlet 5 *loved* lovèd 9 *most* must

I, vii, 6 *shoal* Schoole 47 *do* no

II, i, 20 *weird* weyward 55 *strides* sides 56 *sure* sowre 57 *way they* they may

II, ii, 13 s.d. *Enter Macbeth* (appears after line 8 in folio)

III, i, 2 *weird* weyard

III, iv, 78 *time* times 133 *weird* weyard 135 *worst. For* worst, for 144 *in deed* indeed

III, vi, 24 *son* Sonnes 38 *the* their

IV, i, 59 *all together* altogether 93 *Dunsinane* Dunsmane 98 *Birnam* Byrnan 111 s.d. *Kings and Banquo, last* Kings, and Banquo last 119 *eighth* eight 136 *weird* weyard

IV, ii, 22 *none* move 30 s.d. *Exit* Exit Rosse 72 s.d. *Exit* Exit Messenger

IV, iii, 4 *downfall'n* downfall   15 *deserve* discerne   107 *accursed* accust   133 *thy here-approach* they here approach   235 *tune* time

V, i, 1 *two* too

V, ii, 5, 31 *Birnam* Byrnan

V, iii, 2, 60 *Birnam* Byrnan   55 *senna* Cyme

V, iv, 3 *Birnam* Byrnan   11 *gone* given

V, v, 34, 44 *Birnam* Byrnan   39 *shalt* shall

V, vii, 19 *unbattered* unbatterèd

V, viii, 30 *Birnam* Byrnan

MACBETH

Duncan, King of Scotland
Malcolm ⎫
Donalbain ⎭ *his sons*
Macbeth ⎫
Banquo ⎪
Macduff ⎪
Lennox ⎪
Ross ⎬ *noblemen of Scotland*
Menteith ⎪
Angus ⎪
Caithness ⎭
Fleance, son to Banquo
Siward, Earl of Northumberland
Young Siward, his son
Seyton, an officer attending on Macbeth
Boy, son to Macduff
A Captain
An English Doctor
A Scottish Doctor
A Porter
An Old Man
Three Murderers
Lady Macbeth
Lady Macduff
A Gentlewoman, attending on Lady Macbeth
The Weird Sisters
Hecate
The Ghost of Banquo
Apparitions
Lords, Officers, Soldiers, Messengers, Attendants

Scene : *Scotland and England*]

MACBETH

Thunder and lightning. Enter three Witches.   I, i

1 WITCH   When shall we three meet again
             In thunder, lightning, or in rain?

2. WITCH   When the hurlyburly's done,
             When the battle's lost and won.

3. WITCH   That will be ere the set of sun.

1. WITCH   Where the place?

2. WITCH   Upon the heath.

3. WITCH   There to meet with Macbeth.

1. WITCH   I come, Graymalkin!   8

2. WITCH   Paddock calls.   9

3. WITCH   Anon!

ALL   Fair is foul, and foul is fair.
        Hover through the fog and filthy air.   *Exeunt.*

*

Alarum within. Enter King [Duncan], Malcolm,   I, ii
Donalbain, Lennox, with Attendants, meeting a
bleeding Captain.

KING
     What bloody man is that? He can report,
     As seemeth by his plight, of the revolt
     The newest state.

I, i An open place   8 *Graymalkin* her familiar spirit, a gray cat   9 *Paddock*
a toad; *Anon* at once
I, ii A field near Forres

3 MALCOLM   This is the sergeant
        Who like a good and hardy soldier fought
        'Gainst my captivity. Hail, brave friend!
        Say to the King the knowledge of the broil
        As thou didst leave it.
        CAPTAIN   Doubtful it stood,
        As two spent swimmers that do cling together
        And choke their art. The merciless Macdonwald
        (Worthy to be a rebel, for to that
        The multiplying villainies of nature
12   Do swarm upon him) from the Western Isles
13   Of kerns and gallowglasses is supplied;
        And Fortune, on his damnèd quarrel smiling,
        Showed like a rebel's whore. But all's too weak:
        For brave Macbeth (well he deserves that name),
        Disdaining Fortune, with his brandished steel,
        Which smoked with bloody execution,
19   Like valor's minion carved out his passage
        Till he faced the slave;
        Which ne'er shook hands nor bade farewell to him
22   Till he unseamed him from the nave to th' chops
        And fixed his head upon our battlements.
        KING
        O valiant cousin! worthy gentleman!
        CAPTAIN
        As whence the sun 'gins his reflection
        Shipwracking storms and direful thunders break,
        So from that spring whence comfort seemed to come
        Discomfort swells. Mark, King of Scotland, mark.
        No sooner justice had, with valor armed,
        Compelled these skipping kerns to trust their heels
31   But the Norweyan lord, surveying vantage,
        With furbished arms and new supplies of men,

3 *sergeant* so designated, apparently, as a staff-officer; he ranks as a captain
12 *Western Isles* Hebrides (and Ireland?) 13 *kerns* Irish bush-fighters;
gallowglasses Irish regulars, armored infantrymen 19 *minion* darling 22
nave navel 31 *surveying vantage* seeing opportunity

Began a fresh assault.

KING   Dismayed not this
Our captains, Macbeth and Banquo?

CAPTAIN   Yes,
As sparrows eagles, or the hare the lion.
If I say sooth, I must report they were
As cannons overcharged with double cracks,   37
So they doubly redoubled strokes upon the foe.
Except they meant to bathe in reeking wounds,
Or memorize another Golgotha,   40
I cannot tell—
But I am faint; my gashes cry for help.

KING
So well thy words become thee as thy wounds,
They smack of honor both. Go get him surgeons.
                              [*Exit Captain, attended.*]
     Enter Ross and Angus.
Who comes here?

MALCOLM   The worthy Thane of Ross.   45

LENNOX
What a haste looks through his eyes! So should he look
That seems to speak things strange.   47

ROSS   God save the King!

KING
Whence cam'st thou, worthy Thane?

ROSS   From Fife, great King,
Where the Norweyan banners flout the sky
And fan our people cold.
Norway himself, with terrible numbers,
Assisted by that most disloyal traitor
The Thane of Cawdor, began a dismal conflict,   53
Till that Bellona's bridegroom, lapped in proof,   54
Confronted him with self-comparisons,   55

37 *cracks* explosives   40 *memorize another Golgotha* make memorable as
another 'place of the dead'   45 *Thane* a Scottish lord   47 *seems to* seems
about to   53 *dismal* ominous   54 *Bellona* goddess of war; *lapped in proof*
clad in proven armor   55 *self-comparisons* cancelling powers

27

Point against point rebellious, arm 'gainst arm,
Curbing his lavish spirit : and to conclude,
The victory fell on us.

KING   Great happiness !

ROSS   That now
59   Sweno, the Norways' king, craves composition ;
     Nor would we deign him burial of his men
61   Till he disbursèd, at Saint Colme's Inch,
62   Ten thousand dollars to our general use.

KING
     No more that Thane of Cawdor shall deceive
64   Our bosom interest. Go pronounce his present death
     And with his former title greet Macbeth.

ROSS
     I'll see it done.

KING
     What he hath lost noble Macbeth hath won.   *Exeunt.*

*

I, iii   *Thunder. Enter the three Witches.*
     1 . WITCH Where hast thou been, sister ?
     2 . WITCH Killing swine.
     3 . WITCH Sister, where thou ?
     1 . WITCH A sailor's wife had chestnuts in her lap
                And mounched and mounched and mounched.
                'Give me,' quoth I.
6   'Aroint thee, witch !' the rump-fed ronyon
                cries.
                Her husband 's to Aleppo gone, master o' th'
                Tiger :
                But in a sieve I'll thither sail

59 *composition* terms of surrender   61 *Inch* island   62 *dollars* Spanish or
Dutch coins   64 *bosom interest* heart's trust
I, iii A heath   6 *Aroint thee* get thee gone; *rump-fed ronyon* fat-rumped
scab

And, like a rat without a tail,
I'll do, I'll do, and I'll do.
2. WITCH I'll give thee a wind.
1. WITCH Th' art kind.
3. WITCH And I another.
1. WITCH I myself have all the other,
And the very ports they blow,   15
All the quarters that they know
I' th' shipman's card.   17
I'll drain him dry as hay.
Sleep shall neither night nor day
Hang upon his penthouse lid.   20
He shall live a man forbid.   21
Weary sev'nights, nine times nine,
Shall he dwindle, peak, and pine.
Though his bark cannot be lost,
Yet it shall be tempest-tost.
Look what I have.
2. WITCH Show me, show me.
1. WITCH Here I have a pilot's thumb,
Wracked as homeward he did come.
Drum within.
3. WITCH A drum, a drum!
Macbeth doth come.
ALL The weird sisters, hand in hand,   32
Posters of the sea and land,   33
Thus do go about, about,
Thrice to thine, and thrice to mine,
And thrice again, to make up nine.
Peace! The charm's wound up.
Enter Macbeth and Banquo.
MACBETH
So foul and fair a day I have not seen.

---

15 *very ports they blow* i.e. their power to blow ships to ports   17 *card* compass card   20 *penthouse lid* eyelid   21 *forbid* accursed   32 *weird* fate-serving   33 *Posters* swift travellers

BANQUO
How far is't called to Forres? What are these,
So withered and so wild in their attire
That look not like th' inhabitants o' th' earth
And yet are on't? Live you, or are you aught
43 That man may question? You seem to understand me,
44 By each at once her choppy finger laying
Upon her skinny lips. You should be women,
And yet your beards forbid me to interpret
That you are so.
MACBETH   Speak, if you can. What are you?
1 . WITCH
All hail, Macbeth! Hail to thee, Thane of Glamis!
2 . WITCH
All hail, Macbeth! Hail to thee, Thane of Cawdor!
3 . WITCH
All hail, Macbeth, that shalt be King hereafter!
BANQUO
Good sir, why do you start and seem to fear
Things that do sound so fair? I' th' name of truth,
53 Are ye fantastical, or that indeed
Which outwardly ye show? My noble partner
55 You greet with present grace and great prediction
Of noble having and of royal hope,
57 That he seems rapt withal. To me you speak not.
58 If you can look into the seeds of time
And say which grain will grow and which will not,
Speak then to me, who neither beg nor fear
Your favors nor your hate.
1 . WITCH Hail!
2 . WITCH Hail!
3 . WITCH Hail!
1 . WITCH
Lesser than Macbeth, and greater.

---

43 *question* confer with   44 *choppy* chapped   53 *fantastical* creatures of
fantasy   55 *grace* honor   57 *rapt withal* spellbound at the thought   58
seeds of time genesis of events

2. WITCH

Not so happy, yet much happier.   66

3. WITCH

Thou shalt get kings, though thou be none.   67
So all hail, Macbeth and Banquo!

1. WITCH

Banquo and Macbeth, all hail!

MACBETH

Stay, you imperfect speakers, tell me more: 70
By Sinel's death I know I am Thane of Glamis,   71
But how of Cawdor? The Thane of Cawdor lives,
A prosperous gentleman; and to be King
Stands not within the prospect of belief,
No more than to be Cawdor. Say from whence
You owe this strange intelligence, or why
Upon this blasted heath you stop our way
With such prophetic greeting. Speak, I charge you.

                                          Witches vanish.

BANQUO

The earth hath bubbles as the water has,
And these are of them. Whither are they vanished?

MACBETH

Into the air, and what seemed corporal melted   81
As breath into the wind. Would they had stayed!

BANQUO

Were such things here as we do speak about?
Or have we eaten on the insane root   84
That takes the reason prisoner?

MACBETH

Your children shall be kings.

BANQUO   You shall be King.

MACBETH

And Thane of Cawdor too. Went it not so?

BANQUO

To th' selfsame tune and words. Who's here?

66 *happy* fortunate   67 *get* beget   70 *imperfect* incomplete   71 *Sinel* i.e.
Macbeth's father   81 *corporal* corporeal   84 *insane* madness-inducing

Enter Ross and Angus.

ROSS

The King hath happily received, Macbeth,

90   The news of thy success ; and when he reads
Thy personal venture in the rebels' fight,

92   His wonders and his praises do contend
Which should be thine or his. Silenced with that,
In viewing o'er the rest o' th' selfsame day,
He finds thee in the stout Norweyan ranks,
Nothing afeard of what thyself didst make,

97   Strange images of death. As thick as tale

98   Came post with post, and every one did bear
Thy praises in his kingdom's great defense
And poured them down before him.

ANGUS   We are sent

To give thee from our royal master thanks ;
Only to herald thee into his sight,
Not pay thee.

ROSS

And for an earnest of a greater honor,
He bade me, from him, call thee Thane of Cawdor ;

106   In which addition, hail, most worthy Thane,
For it is thine.

BANQUO   What, can the devil speak true ?

MACBETH

The Thane of Cawdor lives. Why do you dress me
In borrowed robes ?

ANGUS   Who was the Thane lives yet,

But under heavy judgment bears that life

111   Which he deserves to lose. Whether he was combined

112   With those of Norway, or did line the rebel

113   With hidden help and vantage, or that with both
He labored in his country's wrack, I know not ;

---

90 *reads* considers   **92–93** *His wonders . . . or his* i.e. dumbstruck admiration
makes him keep your praises to himself   **97** *thick as tale* i.e. as fast as they
can be counted   **98** *post with post* messenger after messenger   **106** *addition*
title   **111** *combined* leagued   **112** *line* support   **113** *vantage* assistance

But treasons capital, confessed and proved,
Have overthrown him.

MACBETH [aside]   Glamis, and Thane of Cawdor –
The greatest is behind!   117
          [To Ross and Angus] Thanks for your pains.
          [Aside to Banquo]
Do you not hope your children shall be kings,
When those that gave the Thane of Cawdor to me
Promised no less to them?

BANQUO [to Macbeth]   That, trusted home,   120
Might yet enkindle you unto the crown,
Besides the Thane of Cawdor. But 'tis strange:
And oftentimes, to win us to our harm,
The instruments of darkness tell us truths,
Win us with honest trifles, to betray's
In deepest consequence.   126
Cousins, a word, I pray you.   127

MACBETH [aside]   Two truths are told,
As happy prologues to the swelling act   128
Of the imperial theme. – I thank you, gentlemen.
          [Aside]
This supernatural soliciting   130
Cannot be ill, cannot be good. If ill,
Why hath it given me earnest of success,
Commencing in a truth? I am Thane of Cawdor.
If good, why do I yield to that suggestion
Whose horrid image doth unfix my hair   *medusa*
And make my seated heart knock at my ribs   136
Against the use of nature? Present fears   137
Are less than horrible imaginings.
My thought, whose murder yet is but fantastical,   139
Shakes so my single state of man that function   140

---

117 *is behind* is to come   120 *home* all the way   126 *deepest consequence* i.e.
in the vital sequel   127 *Cousins* i.e. fellow lords   128–29 *swelling act* . . .
imperial theme i.e. stately drama of rise to sovereignty   130 *soliciting*
inviting, beckoning   136 *seated* fixed   137 *use* way   139 *fantastical*
imaginary   140 *single* unaided, weak; *function* normal powers

Is smothered in surmise and nothing is
But what is not.

142 BANQUO   Look how our partner's rapt.

MACBETH *[aside]*
If chance will have me King, why chance may crown me
Without my stir.

BANQUO   New honors come upon him,
145 Like our strange garments, cleave not to their mould
But with the aid of use.

MACBETH *[aside]*   Come what come may,
Time and the hour runs through the roughest day.

BANQUO
Worthy Macbeth, we stay upon your leisure.

MACBETH
149 Give me your favor. My dull brain was wrought
With things forgotten. Kind gentlemen, your pains
Are regist'red where every day I turn
The leaf to read them. Let us toward the King.
    [Aside to Banquo]
Think upon what hath chanced, and at more time,
The interim having weighed it, let us speak
155 Our free hearts each to other.

BANQUO   Very gladly.

MACBETH
Till then, enough. – Come, friends.   *Exeunt.*

*

I, iv   *Flourish. Enter King [Duncan], Lennox, Malcolm,
               Donalbain, and Attendants.*

KING
Is execution done on Cawdor? Are not
2 Those in commission yet returned?

142 *rapt* bemused   145 *strange* new   149 *favor* pardon   155 *Our free
hearts* our thoughts freely
I, iv A field near Forres as before, or a place in the palace itself   2 *in
commission* commissioned to carry out the execution

MALCOLM   My liege,
They are not yet come back. But I have spoke
With one that saw him die; who did report
That very frankly he confessed his treasons,
Implored your Highness' pardon, and set forth
A deep repentance. Nothing in his life
Became him like the leaving it. He died
As one that had been studied in his death   9
To throw away the dearest thing he owed   10
As 'twere a careless trifle.
KING   There's no art
To find the mind's construction in the face.
He was a gentleman on whom I built
An absolute trust.
       Enter Macbeth, Banquo, Ross, and Angus.
                       O worthiest cousin,
The sin of my ingratitude even now
Was heavy on me. Thou art so far before   16
That swiftest wing of recompense is slow
To overtake thee. Would thou hadst less deserved,
That the proportion both of thanks and payment   19
Might have been mine! Only I have left to say,
More is thy due than more than all can pay.

MACBETH
The service and the loyalty I owe,
In doing it pays itself. Your Highness' part
Is to receive our duties, and our duties
Are to your throne and state children and servants,
Which do but what they should by doing everything
Safe toward your love and honor.   27
KING   Welcome hither.
I have begun to plant thee and will labor   28
To make thee full of growing. Noble Banquo,
That hast no less deserved nor must be known
No less to have done so, let me enfold thee

---

9 *studied* rehearsed   10 *owed* owned   16 *before* ahead in deserving   19
proportion preponderance   27 *Safe* fitting   28 *plant* nurture

And hold thee to my heart.

BANQUO   There if I grow,
The harvest is your own.

KING   My plenteous joys,
34   Wanton in fullness, seek to hide themselves
In drops of sorrow. Sons, kinsmen, thanes,
And you whose places are the nearest, know
We will establish our estate upon
Our eldest, Malcolm, whom we name hereafter
The Prince of Cumberland; which honor must
Not unaccompanied invest him only,
But signs of nobleness, like stars, shall shine
On all deservers. From hence to Inverness,
And bind us further to you.

MACBETH
The rest is labor which is not used for you.
I'll be myself the harbinger, and make joyful
The hearing of my wife with your approach;
So, humbly take my leave.

KING   My worthy Cawdor!

MACBETH [aside]
The Prince of Cumberland – that is a step
On which I must fall down or else o'erleap,
For in my way it lies. Stars, hide your fires;
Let not light see my black and deep desires.
52   The eye wink at the hand; yet let that be
Which the eye fears, when it is done, to see.   Exit.

KING
True, worthy Banquo: he is full so valiant,
And in his commendations I am fed;
It is a banquet to me. Let's after him,
Whose care is gone before to bid us welcome.
It is a peerless kinsman.   Flourish. Exeunt.

*

34 *Wanton* unrestrained   52 *wink at the hand* blind itself to what the hand does

Enter Macbeth's Wife, alone, with a letter.　　　　I, v

LADY *[reads]* 'They met me in the day of success; and I
have learned by the perfect'st report they have more in
them than mortal knowledge. When I burned in desire
to question them further, they made themselves air, into
which they vanished. Whiles I stood rapt in the wonder
of it, came missives from the King, who all-hailed me　6
Thane of Cawdor, by which title, before, these weird
sisters saluted me, and referred me to the coming on of
time with "Hail, King that shalt be!" This have I
thought good to deliver thee, my dearest partner of
greatness, that thou mightst not lose the dues of rejoic-
ing by being ignorant of what greatness is promised
thee. Lay it to thy heart, and farewell.'

Glamis thou art, and Cawdor, and shalt be
What thou art promised. Yet do I fear thy nature.
It is too full o' th' milk of human kindness
To catch the nearest way. Thou wouldst be great,
Art not without ambition, but without
The illness should attend it. What thou wouldst highly, 18
That wouldst thou holily; wouldst not play false,
And yet wouldst wrongly win. Thou'ldst have, great
　　Glamis,
That which cries 'Thus thou must do' if thou have it;
And that which rather thou dost fear to do
Than wishest should be undone. Hie thee hither,
That I may pour my spirits in thine ear
And chastise with the valor of my tongue
All that impedes thee from the golden round　　　26
Which fate and metaphysical aid doth seem　　　27
To have thee crowned withal.　　　　　　　　　28
　　　Enter Messenger.　　　What is your tidings?
MESSENGER
　　The King comes here to-night.

I, v Within Macbeth's castle at Inverness　6 *missives* messengers　18 *illness*
ruthlessness　26 *round* crown　27 *metaphysical* supernatural　28 *withal* with

LADY   Thou'rt mad to say it!
Is not thy master with him? who, were't so,
Would have informed for preparation.

MESSENGER
So please you, it is true. Our Thane is coming.
One of my fellows had the speed of him,
34   Who, almost dead for breath, had scarcely more
Than would make up his message.

LADY   Give him tending;
He brings great news.   *Exit Messenger.*
                The raven himself is hoarse
That croaks the fatal entrance of Duncan
Under my battlements. Come, you spirits
39   That tend on mortal thoughts, unsex me here,
And fill me from the crown to the toe top-full
Of direst cruelty. Make thick my blood;
42   Stop up th' access and passage to remorse,
43   That no compunctious visitings of nature
44   Shake my fell purpose nor keep peace between
Th' effect and it. Come to my woman's breasts
46   And take my milk for gall, you murd'ring ministers,
47   Wherever in your sightless substances
48   You wait on nature's mischief. Come, thick night,
49   And pall thee in the dunnest smoke of hell,
That my keen knife see not the wound it makes,
Nor heaven peep through the blanket of the dark
To cry 'Hold, hold!'
        Enter Macbeth. Great Glamis! worthy Cawdor!
Greater than both, by the all-hail hereafter!
Thy letters have transported me beyond
55   This ignorant present, and I feel now
The future in the instant.

---

34 *breath* want of breath   39 *mortal* deadly   42 *remorse* pity   43 *nature* natural feeling   44 *fell* fierce   44–45 *keep peace . . . and it* i.e. lull it from achieving its end   46 *for gall* in exchange for gall; *ministers* agents   47 *sightless* invisible   48 *wait on* aid   49 *pall thee* shroud thyself; *dunnest* darkest   55 *ignorant* i.e. ordinarily unaware

MACBETH   My dearest love,
Duncan comes here to-night.
LADY   And when goes hence?
MACBETH
  To-morrow, as he purposes.
LADY   O, never
  Shall sun that morrow see!
  Your face, my Thane, is as a book where men
  May read strange matters. To beguile the time,   61
  Look like the time; bear welcome in your eye,   62
  Your hand, your tongue; look like th' innocent flower,
  But be the serpent under't. He that's coming
  Must be provided for; and you shall put
  This night's great business into my dispatch,   66
  Which shall to all our nights and days to come
  Give solely sovereign sway and masterdom.
MACBETH
  We will speak further.
LADY   Only look up clear.   69
  To alter favor ever is to fear.   70
  Leave all the rest to me.   *Exeunt.*

*

Hautboys and torches. Enter King [Duncan],   I, vi
Malcolm, Donalbain, Banquo, Lennox, Macduff,
Ross, Angus, and Attendants.

KING
  This castle hath a pleasant seat. The air   1
  Nimbly and sweetly recommends itself
  Unto our gentle senses.   3
BANQUO   This guest of summer,

61 *beguile the time* make sly use of the occasion   62 *Look like the time* play
up to the occasion   66 *dispatch* swift management   69 *look up clear* appear
untroubled   70 *alter favor* change countenance; *fear* incur risk
I, vi At the portal of Inverness   s.d. *Hautboys* oboes   1 *seat* site   3 *gentle*
soothed

4 The temple-haunting martlet, does approve
5 By his loved mansionry that the heaven's breath
6 Smells wooingly here. No jutty, frieze,
7 Buttress, nor coign of vantage, but this bird
8 Hath made his pendent bed and procreant cradle.
  Where they most breed and haunt, I have observed
  The air is delicate.
    Enter Lady [Macbeth].

KING   See, see, our honored hostess!
11 The love that follows us sometime is our trouble,
  Which still we thank as love. Herein I teach you
13 How you shall bid God 'ield us for your pains
  And thank us for your trouble.

LADY   All our service
  In every point twice done, and then done double,
  Were poor and single business to contend
  Against those honors deep and broad wherewith
  Your Majesty loads our house. For those of old,
  And the late dignities heaped up to them,
20 We rest your hermits.

KING   Where's the Thane of Cawdor?
  We coursed him at the heels and had a purpose
22 To be his purveyor; but he rides well,
  And his great love, sharp as his spur, hath holp him
  To his home before us. Fair and noble hostess,
  We are your guest to-night.

LADY   Your servants ever
26 Have theirs, themselves, and what is theirs, in compt,
  To make their audit at your Highness' pleasure,
28 Still to return your own.

KING   Give me your hand.

---

4 *temple-haunting* nesting in church spires; *martlet* martin, swallow; *approve* prove 5 *loved mansionry* beloved nests 6 *jutty* projection 7 *coign of vantage* convenient corner 8 *procreant* breeding 11-12 *The love . . . as love* the love that sometimes inconveniences us we still hold precious 13 *God 'ield us* God reward me 20 *hermits* beadsmen 22 *purveyor* advance agent of supplies 26 *Have theirs* have their servants; *what is theirs* their possessions; *in compt* in trust 28 *Still* always

Conduct me to mine host ; we love him highly.
And shall continue our graces towards him.
By your leave, hostess.   *Exeunt.*

*

Hautboys. Torches. Enter a Sewer, and divers   I, vii
Servants with dishes and service over the stage. Then
enter Macbeth.

MACBETH

If it were done when 'tis done, then 'twere well	1
It were done quickly. If th' assassination	
Could trammel up the consequence, and catch	3
With his surcease success, that but this blow	4
Might be the be-all and the end-all – ; here,	
But here upon this bank and shoal of time,	
We'ld jump the life to come. But in these cases	7
We still have judgment here, that we but teach	
Bloody instructions, which, being taught, return	9
To plague th' inventor. This even-handed justice	
Commends th' ingredience of our poisoned chalice	
To our own lips. He's here in double trust :	
First, as I am his kinsman and his subject,	
Strong both against the deed ; then, as his host,	
Who should against his murderer shut the door,	
Not bear the knife myself. Besides, this Duncan	
Hath borne his faculties so meek, hath been	17
So clear in his great office, that his virtues	18
Will plead like angels, trumpet-tongued against	
The deep damnation of his taking-off ;	
And pity, like a naked new-born babe	
Striding the blast, or heaven's cherubin horsed	

I, vii The courtyard of Inverness from which open the chambers of the castle   s.d. *Sewer* chief waiter   1 *done* done with   3 *trammel up the consequence* enclose the consequences in a net   4 *his surcease* its (the assassination's) completion; *success* all that follows   7 *jump* risk   9 *instructions* lessons   17 *faculties* powers   18 *clear* untainted

23   Upon the sightless couriers of the air,
        Shall blow the horrid deed in every eye
        That tears shall drown the wind. I have no spur
        To prick the sides of my intent, but only
        Vaulting ambition, which o'erleaps itself
        And falls on th' other –
                Enter Lady [Macbeth].
                                How now? What news?
LADY
        He has almost supped. Why have you left the chamber?
MACBETH
        Hath he asked for me?
LADY   Know you not he has?
MACBETH
        We will proceed no further in this business.
32   He hath honored me of late, and I have bought
        Golden opinions from all sorts of people,
        Which would be worn now in their newest gloss,
        Not cast aside so soon.
LADY   Was the hope drunk
        Wherein you dressed yourself? Hath it slept since?
37   And wakes it now to look so green and pale
        At what it did so freely? From this time
        Such I account thy love. Art thou afeard
        To be the same in thine own act and valor
        As thou art in desire? Wouldst thou have that
        Which thou esteem'st the ornament of life,
        And live a coward in thine own esteem,
        Letting 'I dare not' wait upon 'I would,'
45   Like the poor cat i' th' adage?
MACBETH   Prithee peace!
        I dare do all that may become a man;
        Who dares do more is none.
LADY   What beast was't then

23 *sightless couriers* invisible coursers (the winds)   32 *bought* acquired   37
green bilious   45 *cat i' th' adage* (who wants the fish but doesn't want to get
its paws wet)

That made you break this enterprise to me ?   48
When you durst do it, then you were a man ;
And to be more than what you were, you would
Be so much more the man. Nor time nor place
Did then adhere, and yet you would make both.   52
They have made themselves, and that their fitness now 53
Does unmake you. I have given suck, and know
How tender 'tis to love the babe that milks me :
I would, while it was smiling in my face,
Have plucked my nipple from his boneless gums
And dashed the brains out, had I so sworn as you
Have done to this.

MACBETH   If we should fail ?
LADY   We fail ?
But screw your courage to the sticking place   60
And we'll not fail. When Duncan is asleep
(Whereto the rather shall his day's hard journey
Soundly invite him), his two chamberlains
Will I with wine and wassail so convince   64
That memory, the warder of the brain,
Shall be a fume, and the receipt of reason   66
A limbeck only. When in swinish sleep   67
Their drenchèd natures lies as in a death,
What cannot you and I perform upon
Th' unguarded Duncan ? what not put upon
His spongy officers, who shall bear the guilt
Of our great quell ?   72
MACBETH   Bring forth men-children only ;
For thy undaunted mettle should compose   73
Nothing but males. Will it not be received,
When we have marked with blood those sleepy two
Of his own chamber and used their very daggers,

---

48 *break* broach   52 *adhere* lend themselves to the occasion   53 *that their fitness* their very fitness   60 *sticking place* notch (holding the string of a crossbow cranked taut for shooting)   64 *convince* overcome   66 *receipt* container   67 *limbeck* cap of a still (to which the fumes rise)   72 *quell* killing   73 *mettle* vital substance

That they have done't?

77 LADY   Who dares receive it other,
As we shall make our griefs and clamor roar
Upon his death?

MACBETH   I am settled, and bend up
Each corporal agent to this terrible feat.

81   Away, and mock the time with fairest show;
False face must hide what the false heart doth know.

Exeunt.

                              *

II, i   *Enter Banquo, and Fleance, with a torch before him.*

BANQUO
How goes the night, boy?

FLEANCE
The moon is down; I have not heard the clock.

BANQUO
And she goes down at twelve.

FLEANCE   I take't, 'tis later, sir.

BANQUO
4   Hold, take my sword. There's husbandry in heaven;
Their candles are all out. Take thee that too.

6   A heavy summons lies like lead upon me,
And yet I would not sleep. Merciful powers,
Restrain in me the cursèd thoughts that nature
Gives way to in repose.
             Enter Macbeth, and a Servant with a torch.
                              Give me my sword!

Who's there?

MACBETH
A friend.

BANQUO
What, sir, not yet at rest? The King's abed.
He hath been in unusual pleasure and

77 *other* otherwise   81 *mock* delude
II, i The same   4 *husbandry* economy   6 *summons* signal to sleep

44

Sent forth great largess to your offices.   14
This diamond he greets your wife withal
By the name of most kind hostess, and shut up   16
In measureless content.

MACBETH   Being unprepared,
Our will became the servant to defect,   18
Which else should free have wrought.

BANQUO   All's well.
I dreamt last night of the three weird sisters.
To you they have showed some truth.

MACBETH   I think not of them.
Yet when we can entreat an hour to serve,
We would spend it in some words upon that business,
If you would grant the time.

BANQUO   At your kind'st leisure.

MACBETH
If you shall cleave to my consent, when 'tis,   25
It shall make honor for you.

BANQUO   So I lose none
In seeking to augment it, but still keep
My bosom franchised and allegiance clear,   28
I shall be counselled.   -9

MACBETH   Good repose the while.

BANQUO
Thanks, sir. The like to you.

Exeunt Banquo [and Fleance].

MACBETH
Go bid thy mistress, when my drink is ready,
She strike upon the bell. Get thee to bed. *Exit [Servant].*
Is this a dagger which I see before me,
The handle toward my hand? Come, let me clutch thee!
I have thee not, and yet I see thee still.
Art thou not, fatal vision, sensible

---

14 *largess to your offices* gratuities to your household departments   16 *shut
up* concluded   18 *will* good will; *defect* deficient means   25 *cleave...when
'tis* favor my cause at the proper time   28 *franchised* free from guilt   29
counselled open to persuasion

To feeling as to sight ? or art thou but
A dagger of the mind, a false creation
Proceeding from the heat–oppressèd brain ?
I see thee yet, in form as palpable
As this which now I draw.
Thou marshall'st me the way that I was going,
And such an instrument I was to use.
Mine eyes are made the fools o' th' other senses,
Or else worth all the rest. I see thee still,

46   And on thy blade and dudgeon gouts of blood,
Which was not so before. There's no such thing.

48   It is the bloody business which informs
Thus to mine eyes. Now o'er the one half-world

50   Nature seems dead, and wicked dreams abuse
The curtained sleep. Witchcraft celebrates

52   Pale Hecate's offerings ; and withered murder,

53   Alarumed by his sentinel, the wolf,
Whose howl 's his watch, thus with his stealthy pace,

55   With Tarquin's ravishing strides, towards his design
Moves like a ghost. Thou sure and firm-set earth,
Hear not my steps which way they walk, for fear
Thy very stones prate of my whereabout

59   And take the present horror from the time,
Which now suits with it. Whiles I threat, he lives ;
Words to the heat of deeds too cold breath gives.
        A bell rings.
I go, and it is done. The bell invites me.
Hear it not, Duncan, for it is a knell
That summons thee to heaven, or to hell.   *Exit.*

II, ii   *Enter Lady [Macbeth].*

LADY
That which hath made them drunk hath made me bold ;

46 *dudgeon* wooden hilt; *gouts* blobs   48 *informs* creates impressions   50
abuse deceive   52 *Hecate's offerings* worship of Hecate (Goddess of sorcery)
53 *Alarumed* given the signal   55 *Tarquin* Roman tyrant, ravisher of
Lucrece   59–60 *take . . . suits with it* delay, by prating, the commission of
the deed at this suitably horrible moment (?), reduce, by breaking the
silence, the suitable horror of this moment (?)

What hath quenched them hath given me fire. Hark!
  Peace!
It was the owl that shrieked, the fatal bellman   3
Which gives the stern'st good-night. He is about it.
The doors are open, and the surfeited grooms
Do mock their charge with snores. I have drugged their   6
  possets,
That death and nature do contend about them
Whether they live or die.

MACBETH [within]   Who's there? What, ho?

LADY
  Alack, I am afraid they have awaked,
  And 'tis not done! Th' attempt, and not the deed,
  Confounds us. Hark! I laid their daggers ready –   11
  He could not miss 'em. Had he not resembled
  My father as he slept, I had done't.
          Enter Macbeth.   My husband!

MACBETH
  I have done the deed. Didst thou not hear a noise?

LADY
  I heard the owl scream and the crickets cry.
  Did not you speak?

MACBETH   When?

LADY   Now.

MACBETH   As I descended?

LADY Ay.

MACBETH Hark!
  Who lies i' th' second chamber?

LADY   Donalbain.

MACBETH This is a sorry sight.

LADY
  A foolish thought, to say a sorry sight.

MACBETH
  There's one did laugh in's sleep, and one cried 'Murder!'

II, ii   3–4 *fatal bellman . . . good-night* i.e. like the night-watch cry to felons
scheduled for execution in the morning   6 *possets* bedtime drinks   11
Confounds ruins

23 That they did wake each other. I stood and heard them.
    But they did say their prayers and addressed them
    Again to sleep.

LADY   There are two lodged together.

MACBETH
    One cried 'God bless us!' and 'Amen!' the other,
27 As they had seen me with these hangman's hands,
    List'ning their fear. I could not say 'Amen!'
    When they did say 'God bless us!'

LADY   Consider it not so deeply.

MACBETH
    But wherefore could not I pronounce 'Amen'?
    I had most need of blessing, and 'Amen'
    Stuck in my throat.

LADY   These deeds must not be thought
    After these ways; so, it will make us mad.

MACBETH
    Methought I heard a voice cry 'Sleep no more!
    Macbeth does murder sleep' – the innocent sleep,
36 Sleep that knits up the ravelled sleave of care,
    The death of each day's life, sore labor's bath,
38 Balm of hurt minds, great nature's second course,
    Chief nourisher in life's feast.

LADY   What do you mean?

MACBETH
    Still it cried 'Sleep no more!' to all the house;
    'Glamis hath murdered sleep, and therefore Cawdor
    Shall sleep no more, Macbeth shall sleep no more.'

LADY
    Who was it that thus cried? Why, worthy Thane,
44 You do unbend your noble strength to think
    So brainsickly of things. Go get some water
46 And wash this filthy witness from your hand.

---

23 *That* so that   27 *hangman's hands* i.e. bloody, like an executioner's   36
knits up . . . sleave smooths out the tangled skein   38 *second course* i.e. sleep,
after food   44 *unbend* relax   46 *witness* evidence

Why did you bring these daggers from the place?
They must lie there: go carry them and smear
The sleepy grooms with blood.

MACBETH   I'll go no more.
I am afraid to think what I have done;
Look on't again I dare not.

LADY   Infirm of purpose!
Give me the daggers. The sleeping and the dead
Are but as pictures. 'Tis the eye of childhood   53
That fears a painted devil. If he do bleed,
I'll gild the faces of the grooms withal,   55
For it must seem their guilt.   *Exit.*
   Knock within.

MACBETH
Whence is that knocking?
How is't with me when every noise appals me?
What hands are here? Ha! they pluck out mine eyes.
Will all great Neptune's ocean wash this blood
Clean from my hand? No, this my hand will rather
The multitudinous seas incarnadine,   61
Making the green one red.   62
   Enter Lady [Macbeth].

LADY
My hands are of your color, but I shame
To wear a heart so white. *(Knock.)* I hear a knocking
At the south entry. Retire we to our chamber.
A little water clears us of this deed.
How easy is it then! Your constancy
Hath left you unattended.   68
  Knock.   Hark! more knocking.
Get on your nightgown, lest occasion call us   69
And show us to be watchers. Be not lost   70
So poorly in your thoughts.   71

---

53 *as pictures* like pictures (since without motion) 55 *gild* paint 61
incarnadine redden 62 *one* uniformly 68 *unattended* deserted 69 *nightgown* dressing gown 70 *watchers* i.e. awake 71 *poorly* weakly

MACBETH
 To know my deed, 'twere best not know myself.
  Knock.
 Wake Duncan with thy knocking! I would thou couldst.
              Exeunt.

II, iii   *Enter a Porter. Knocking within.*

  PORTER Here's a knocking indeed! If a man were porter of
2 hell gate, he should have old turning the key. *(Knock.)*
 Knock, knock, knock. Who's there, i' th' name of Belze-
4 bub? Here's a farmer that hanged himself on th' expecta-
5 tion of plenty. Come in time! Have napkins enow about
 you; here you'll sweat for't. *(Knock.)* Knock, knock.
 Who's there, in th' other devil's name? Faith, here's an
8 equivocator, that could swear in both the scales against
 either scale; who committed treason enough for God's
 sake, yet could not equivocate to heaven. O come in,
 equivocator. *(Knock.)* Knock, knock, knock. Who's
 there? Faith, here's an English tailor come hither for
13 stealing out of a French hose. Come in, tailor. Here you
14 may roast your goose. *(Knock.)* Knock, knock. Never at
 quiet! What are you? – But this place is too cold for hell.
 I'll devil-porter it no further. I had thought to have let
 in some of all professions that go the primrose way to th'
 everlasting bonfire. *(Knock.)* Anon, anon! *[Opens the
 way.]* I pray you remember the porter.
   Enter Macduff and Lennox.

MACDUFF
 Was it so late, friend, ere you went to bed,
 That you do lie so late?
22 PORTER Faith, sir, we were carousing till the second cock;
 and drink, sir, is a great provoker of three things.

II, iii 2 *old* much 4 *farmer* i.e. one who has hoarded crops 4–5 *expectation of plenty* prospect of a crop surplus (which will lower prices) 5 *enow*
enough 8 *equivocator* (usually considered an allusion to the Jesuits tried
for political conspiracy) 13 *French hose* close-fitting breeches 14 *roast
your goose* heat your pressing-iron 22 *second cock* second cockcrow (3 a.m.)

MACDUFF What three things does drink especially pro-
voke?

PORTER Marry, sir, nose-painting, sleep, and urine.
Lechery, sir, it provokes, and unprovokes: it provokes
the desire, but it takes away the performance. Therefore
much drink may be said to be an equivocator with lechery: it makes him, and it mars him; it sets him on, and it
takes him off; it persuades him, and disheartens him;
makes him stand to, and not stand to; in conclusion, 31
equivocates him in a sleep, and, giving him the lie,
leaves him.

MACDUFF I believe drink gave thee the lie last night. 33

PORTER That it did, sir, i' the very throat on me; but I
requited him for his lie; and, I think, being too strong
for him, though he took up my legs sometime, yet I
made a shift to cast him. 37

MACDUFF Is thy master stirring?
        Enter Macbeth.
Our knocking has awaked him: here he comes.

LENNOX
Good morrow, noble sir.

MACBETH   Good morrow, both.

MACDUFF
Is the King stirring, worthy Thane?

MACBETH   Not yet.

MACDUFF
He did command me to call timely on him; 42
I have almost slipped the hour. 43

MACBETH   I'll bring you to him.

MACDUFF
I know this is a joyful trouble to you;
But yet 'tis one.

MACBETH
The labor we delight in physics pain. 46

31 *stand to* stand his guard   33 *gave thee the lie* called you a liar (i.e. unable
to stand)   37 *cast* throw   42 *timely* early   43 *slipped* let slip   46 *physics
pain* cures trouble

This is the door.

MACDUFF   I'll make so bold to call,
48 For 'tis my limited service.   *Exit Macduff.*

LENNOX
Goes the King hence to-day?

MACBETH   He does; he did appoint so.

LENNOX
The night has been unruly. Where we lay,
Our chimneys were blown down; and, as they say,
Lamentings heard i' th' air, strange screams of death,
And prophesying, with accents terrible,
54 Of dire combustion and confused events
55 New hatched to th' woeful time. The obscure bird
Clamored the livelong night. Some say the earth
Was feverous and did shake.

MACBETH   'Twas a rough night.

LENNOX
My young remembrance cannot parallel
A fellow to it.
        Enter Macduff.

MACDUFF
O horror, horror, horror! Tongue nor heart
Cannot conceive nor name thee!

MACBETH AND LENNOX   What's the matter?

MACDUFF
62 Confusion now hath made his masterpiece:
Most sacrilegious murder hath broke ope
The Lord's anointed temple and stole thence
The life o' th' building!

MACBETH   What is't you say? the life?

LENNOX
Mean you his Majesty?

MACDUFF
Approach the chamber and destroy your sight

---

48 *limited* appointed   **54** *combustion* tumult   **55** *obscure bird* i.e. the owl
62 *Confusion* destruction

With a new Gorgon. Do not bid me speak.   68
See, and then speak yourselves.
>   *Exeunt Macbeth and Lennox.*
>   Awake, awake!
Ring the alarum bell! Murder and treason!
Banquo and Donalbain! Malcolm, awake!
Shake off this downy sleep, death's counterfeit,
And look on death itself. Up, up, and see
The great doom's image. Malcolm! Banquo!   74
As from your graves rise up and walk like sprites
To countenance this horror. Ring the bell!   76
>   *Bell rings. Enter Lady [Macbeth].*

LADY
> What's the business,
> That such a hideous trumpet calls to parley
> The sleepers of the house? Speak, speak!

MACDUFF   O gentle lady,
> 'Tis not for you to hear what I can speak:
> The repetition in a woman's ear   81
> Would murder as it fell.
>   *Enter Banquo.*   O Banquo, Banquo,
> Our royal master's murdered!

LADY   Woe, alas!
> What, in our house?

BANQUO   Too cruel anywhere.
> Dear Duff, I prithee contradict thyself
> And say it is not so.
>   *Enter Macbeth, Lennox, and Ross.*

MACBETH
> Had I but died an hour before this chance,
> I had lived a blessèd time; for from this instant
> There's nothing serious in mortality: 89
> All is but toys. Renown and grace is dead,   90

---

68 *a new Gorgon* a new Medusa (capable of turning the beholder's eyes to
stone)   74 *great doom's image* resemblance of the day of judgment   76
countenance appear in keeping with   81 *repetition* recital   89 *serious in
mortality* worthwhile in human life   90 *toys* trifles

91 The wine of life is drawn, and the mere lees
92 Is left this vault to brag of.
       Enter Malcolm and Donalbain.

DONALBAIN
What is amiss?

MACBETH   You are, and do not know't.
The spring, the head, the fountain of your blood
Is stopped, the very source of it is stopped.

MACDUFF
Your royal father's murdered.

MALCOLM   O, by whom?

LENNOX
Those of his chamber, as it seemed, had done't.
98 Their hands and faces were all badged with blood;
So were their daggers, which unwiped we found
Upon their pillows. They stared and were distracted.
No man's life was to be trusted with them.

MACBETH
O, yet I do repent me of my fury
That I did kill them.

MACDUFF   Wherefore did you so?

MACBETH
104 Who can be wise, amazed, temp'rate and furious,
Loyal and neutral, in a moment? No man.
106 The expedition of my violent love
Outrun the pauser, reason. Here lay Duncan,
His silver skin laced with his golden blood;
And his gashed stabs looked like a breach in nature
For ruin's wasteful entrance: there, the murderers,
Steeped in the colors of their trade, their daggers
112 Unmannerly breeched with gore. Who could refrain
That had a heart to love, and in that heart
Courage to make's love known?

LADY   Help me hence, ho!

---

91 *lees* dregs   92 *vault* wine-vault   98 *badged* marked   104 *amazed* confused   106 *expedition* haste   112 *Unmannerly . . . gore* crudely wearing breeches of blood; *refrain* restrain oneself

MACDUFF
  Look to the lady. 115

MALCOLM [aside to Donalbain]
          Why do we hold our tongues,
  That most may claim this argument for ours? 116

DONALBAIN [to Malcolm]
  What should be spoken here,
  Where our fate, hid in an auger hole, 118
  May rush and seize us? Let's away:
  Our tears are not yet brewed.

MALCOLM [to Donalbain]   Nor our strong sorrow
  Upon the foot of motion. 121

BANQUO   Look to the lady.
        [Lady Macbeth is carried out.]
  And when we have our naked frailties hid, 122
  That suffer in exposure, let us meet
  And question this most bloody piece of work, 124
  To know it further. Fears and scruples shake us. 125
  In the great hand of God I stand, and thence
  Against the undivulged pretense I fight 127
  Of treasonous malice.

MACDUFF   And so do I.

ALL   So all.

MACBETH
  Let's briefly put on manly readiness
  And meet i' th' hall together.

ALL   Well contented.
        Exeunt [all but Malcolm and Donalbain].

MALCOLM
  What will you do? Let's not consort with them.
  To show an unfelt sorrow is an office
  Which the false man does easy. I'll to England.

---

115 *Look to* look after 116 *argument for ours* topic as chiefly our concern
118 *auger hole* i.e. any tiny cranny 121 *Upon the foot of motion* yet in motion
122 *frailties hid* bodies clothed 124 *question* discuss 125 *scruples* doubts
127 *undivulged pretense* secret stratagems

DONALBAIN
    To Ireland I. Our separated fortune
    Shall keep us both the safer. Where we are
136 There's daggers in men's smiles; the near in blood,
    The nearer bloody.
    MALCOLM   This murderous shaft that's shot
    Hath not yet lighted, and our safest way
    Is to avoid the aim. Therefore to horse,
    And let us not be dainty of leave-taking
141 But shift away. There's warrant in that theft
    Which steals itself when there's no mercy left.   *Exeunt*.

*

II, iv   *Enter Ross with an Old Man.*
    OLD MAN
    Threescore and ten I can remember well;
    Within the volume of which time I have seen
    Hours dreadful and things strange, but this sore night
4   Hath trifled former knowings.
    ROSS   Ha, good father,
5   Thou seest the heavens, as troubled with man's act,
    Threatens his bloody stage. By th' clock 'tis day,
7   And yet dark night strangles the travelling lamp.
8   Is't night's predominance, or the day's shame,
    That darkness does the face of earth entomb
    When living light should kiss it?
    OLD MAN   'Tis unnatural,
    Even like the deed that's done. On Tuesday last
12 A falcon, tow'ring in her pride of place,
13 Was by a mousing owl hawked at and killed.

---

136 *near* nearer   141 *warrant* justification
II, iv Outside Inverness castle   4 *trifled former knowings* made former
experiences seem trifling   5 *man's act* the human drama   7 *travelling
lamp* i.e. of Phoebus, the sun   8 *predominance* supernatural ascendancy
12 *tow'ring* soaring   13 *mousing* i.e. ordinarily preying on mice; *hawked
at* swooped upon

ROSS
>   And Duncan's horses (a thing most strange and certain),   14
>   Beauteous and swift, the minions of their race,   15
>   Turned wild in nature, broke their stalls, flung out,   16
>   Contending 'gainst obedience, as they would make
>   War with mankind.

OLD MAN   'Tis said they eat each other.   18

ROSS
>   They did so, to th' amazement of mine eyes
>   That looked upon't.
>   *Enter Macduff.* Here comes the good Macduff.
>   How goes the world, sir, now?

MACDUFF   Why, see you not?

ROSS
>   Is't known who did this more than bloody deed?

MACDUFF
>   Those that Macbeth hath slain.

ROSS   Alas the day,
>   What good could they pretend?   24

MACDUFF   They were suborned.
>   Malcolm and Donalbain, the King's two sons,
>   Are stol'n away and fled, which puts upon them
>   Suspicion of the deed.

ROSS   'Gainst nature still.
>   Thriftless ambition, that will ravin up   28
>   Thine own live's means! Then 'tis most like
>   The sovereignty will fall upon Macbeth.

MACDUFF
>   He is already named, and gone to Scone
>   To be invested.   32

ROSS   Where is Duncan's body?

MACDUFF
>   Carried to Colmekill,
>   The sacred storehouse of his predecessors

14 *certain* significant   15 *minions* darlings   16 *flung out* lunged about   18
eat ate   24 *pretend* expect; *suborned* bribed   28 *Thriftless* wasteful; *ravin
up* bolt, swallow   32 *invested* crowned

And guardian of their bones.

ROSS   Will you to Scone?

MACDUFF
No, cousin, I'll to Fife.

ROSS   Well, I will thither.

MACDUFF
Well, may you see things well done there. Adieu,
Lest our old robes sit easier than our new!

ROSS
Farewell, father.

OLD MAN
40   God's benison go with you, and with those
That would make good of bad, and friends of foes.

                      Exeunt omnes.

*

III, i   *Enter Banquo.*

BANQUO
Thou hast it now – King, Cawdor, Glamis, all,
As the weird women promised; and I fear

3   Thou play'dst most foully for't. Yet it was said
4   It should not stand in thy posterity,
But that myself should be the root and father
Of many kings. If there come truth from them

7   (As upon thee, Macbeth, their speeches shine),
Why, by the verities on thee made good,
May they not be my oracles as well

10   And set me up in hope? But hush, no more!
      Sennet sounded. Enter Macbeth as King, Lady
      [Macbeth], Lennox, Ross, Lords, and Attendants.

MACBETH
Here's our chief guest.

LADY   If he had been forgotten,
It had been as a gap in our great feast,

---

40 *benison* blessing
III, i Within the royal palace (at Forres)   3 *foully* cheatingly   4 *stand*
continue as a legacy   7 *shine* are brilliantly substantiated   10 s.d. *Sennet*
trumpet salute

And all-thing unbecoming.   13

MACBETH
To-night we hold a solemn supper, sir,   14
And I'll request your presence.

BANQUO   Let your Highness
Command upon me, to the which my duties
Are with a most indissoluble tie
For ever knit.

MACBETH   Ride you this afternoon?

BANQUO
Ay, my good lord.

MACBETH
We should have else desired your good advice
(Which still hath been both grave and prosperous)   21
In this day's council; but we'll take to-morrow.
Is't far you ride?

BANQUO
As far, my lord, as will fill up the time
'Twixt this and supper. Go not my horse the better,   25
I must become a borrower of the night   26
For a dark hour or twain.

MACBETH   Fail not our feast.

BANQUO
My lord, I will not.

MACBETH
We hear our bloody cousins are bestowed
In England and in Ireland, not confessing
Their cruel parricide, filling their hearers
With strange invention. But of that to-morrow,   32
When therewithal we shall have cause of state   33
Craving us jointly. Hie you to horse. Adieu,
Till you return at night. Goes Fleance with you?

---

13 *all-thing* altogether   **14** *solemn* state   **21** *still* always; *prosperous* profit-
able   **25** *Go not my horse the better* i.e. unless my horse goes faster than
anticipated   **26** *borrower of* i.e. borrower of time from   **32** *invention*
falsehoods   **33–34** *cause . . . jointly* state business requiring our joint
attention

BANQUO
Ay, my good lord. Our time does call upon's.

MACBETH
I wish your horses swift and sure of foot,
And so I do commend you to their backs.
Farewell.   *Exit Banquo.*
Let every man be master of his time
Till seven at night. To make society
The sweeter welcome, we will keep ourself
43 Till supper time alone. While then, God be with you !
                              Exeunt Lords [and others].
44 Sirrah, a word with you. Attend those men
Our pleasure ?

SERVANT
They are, my lord, without the palace gate.

MACBETH
Bring them before us.   *Exit Servant.*
48 To be thus is nothing, but to be safely thus –
49 Our fears in Banquo stick deep,
And in his royalty of nature reigns that
51 Which would be feared. 'Tis much he dares ;
And to that dauntless temper of his mind
He hath a wisdom that doth guide his valor
To act in safety. There is none but he
Whose being I do fear ; and under him
56 My genius is rebuked, as it is said
Mark Antony's was by Caesar. He chid the sisters
When first they put the name of King upon me,
And bade them speak to him. Then, prophet-like,
They hailed him father to a line of kings.
Upon my head they placed a fruitless crown
62 And put a barren sceptre in my gripe,
Thence to be wrenched with an unlineal hand,

---

43 *While* until   44 *Sirrah* form used in addressing inferiors; *Attend* await
48 *but* unless   49 *in Banquo* about Banquo; *stick deep* are deeply imbedded
in me   51 *would be* deserves to be   56 *genius is rebuked* controlling spirit is
daunted   62 *gripe* grasp

No son of mine succeeding. If't be so,
For Banquo's issue have I filed my mind;   65
For them the gracious Duncan have I murdered;
Put rancors in the vessel of my peace   67
Only for them, and mine eternal jewel   68
Given to the common enemy of man   69
To make them kings – the seeds of Banquo kings.
Rather than so, come, Fate, into the list,   71
And champion me to th' utterance! Who's there?   72
        Enter Servant and two Murderers.
Now go to the door and stay there till we call.
                                        Exit Servant.

Was it not yesterday we spoke together?
MURDERERS
It was, so please your Highness.
MACBETH   Well then, now
Have you considered of my speeches? Know
That it was he, in the times past, which held you
So under fortune, which you thought had been   78
Our innocent self. This I made good to you
In our last conference, passed in probation with you   80
How you were borne in hand, how crossed; the   81
    instruments;
Who wrought with them; and all things else that might
To half a soul and to a notion crazed   83
Say 'Thus did Banquo.'
1. MURDERER   You made it known to us.
MACBETH
I did so; and went further, which is now
Our point of second meeting. Do you find   86
Your patience so predominant in your nature

65 *filed* defiled 67 *rancors* bitter enmities 68 *jewel* soul 69 *common enemy of man* i.e. Satan 71 *list* lists, field of combat 72 *champion . . . utterance* engage with me to the death 78 *under fortune* out of favor with fortune 80 *passed in probation* reviewed the evidence 81 *borne in hand* manipulated; *crossed* thwarted; *instruments* agents 83 *half a soul* a halfwit; *notion* mind 86 *Our point of* the point of our

88   That you can let this go ? Are you so gospelled
      To pray for this good man and for his issue,
      Whose heavy hand hath bowed you to the grave
      And beggared yours for ever ?
      1. MURDERER   We are men, my liege.
      MACBETH
92   Ay, in the catalogue ye go for men,
      As hounds and greyhounds, mongrels, spaniels, curs,
94   Shoughs, water-rugs, and demi-wolves are clept
95   All by the name of dogs. The valued file
      Distinguishes the swift, the slow, the subtle,
97   The housekeeper, the hunter, every one
      According to the gift which bounteous nature
99   Hath in him closed, whereby he does receive
100   Particular addition, from the bill
      That writes them all alike ; and so of men.
      Now, if you have a station in the file,
      Not i' th' worst rank of manhood, say't ;
104   And I will put that business in your bosoms
      Whose execution takes your enemy off,
      Grapples you to the heart and love of us,
      Who wear our health but sickly in his life,
      Which in his death were perfect.
      2. MURDERER   I am one, my liege,
      Whom the vile blows and buffets of the world
      Have so incensed that I am reckless what
      I do to spite the world.
      1. MURDERER   And I another,
      So weary with disasters, tugged with fortune,
113   That I would set my life on any chance
      To mend it or be rid on't.

---

88 *gospelled* tamed by gospel precepts   92 *catalogue* inventory, classification   94 *Shoughs* shaggy pet dogs; *water-rugs* long-haired water-dogs; *clept*
named   95 *valued file* classification according to valuable traits   97 *housekeeper* watchdog   99 *closed* invested   100 *addition, from the bill* distinction,
contrary to the listing   104 *in your bosoms* in your trust   113 *set* risk

MACBETH   Both of you
  Know Banquo was your enemy.
MURDERERS   True, my lord.
MACBETH
  So is he mine, and in such bloody distance   116
  That every minute of his being thrusts
  Against my near'st of life ; and though I could   118
  With barefaced power sweep him from my sight
  And bid my will avouch it, yet I must not,   120
  For certain friends that are both his and mine,   121
  Whose loves I may not drop, but wail his fall   122
  Who I myself struck down. And thence it is
  That I to your assistance do make love,
  Masking the business from the common eye
  For sundry weighty reasons.
2. MURDERER   We shall, my lord,
  Perform what you command us.
1. MURDERER   Though our lives –
MACBETH
  Your spirits shine through you. Within this hour at most
  I will advise you where to plant yourselves,
  Acquaint you with the perfect spy o' th' time   130
  The moment on't, for't must be done to-night
  And something from the palace (always thought   132
  That I require a clearness) ; and with him,   133
  To leave no rubs nor botches in the work,   134
  Fleance his son, that keeps him company,
  Whose absence is no less material to me
  Than is his father's, must embrace the fate
  Of that dark hour. Resolve yourselves apart ;
  I'll come to you anon.
MURDERERS   We are resolved, my lord.

---

116 *distance* enmity   118 *near'st of life* vital parts   120 *avouch* justify   121
For because of   122 *wail* I must wail   130 *with the perfect spy o' th' time*
by means of a perfect look-out (?), with precise timing (?)   132 *thought*
borne in mind   133 *clearness* alibi   134 *rubs* defects

MACBETH
> I'll call upon you straight. Abide within.
> It is concluded. Banquo, thy soul's flight,
> If it find heaven, must find it out to-night.   *Exeunt.*

*

III, ii   *Enter Macbeth's Lady and a Servant.*

LADY
> Is Banquo gone from court?

SERVANT
> Ay, madam, but returns again to-night.

LADY
> Say to the King I would attend his leisure
> For a few words.

SERVANT   Madam, I will.   *Exit.*

LADY   Naught's had, all's spent,
> Where our desire is got without content.
> 'Tis safer to be that which we destroy
> Than by destruction dwell in doubtful joy.
>   *Enter Macbeth.*
> How now, my lord? Why do you keep alone,
9   Of sorriest fancies your companions making,
>   Using those thoughts which should indeed have died
11 With them they think on? Things without all remedy
>   Should be without regard. What's done is done.

MACBETH
13 We have scorched the snake, not killed it.
14 She'll close and be herself, whilst our poor malice
>   Remains in danger of her former tooth.
16 But let the frame of things disjoint, both the worlds
>   suffer,
>   Ere we will eat our meal in fear, and sleep

III, ii The same   9 *sorriest* most contemptible   11 *all remedy* any form of remedy   13 *scorched* slashed   14 *close* heal; *poor malice* feeble opposition   16 *frame of things disjoint* structure of the universe collapse; *both the worlds* i.e. heaven and earth

In the affliction of these terrible dreams
That shake us nightly. Better be with the dead,
Whom we, to gain our peace, have sent to peace,
Than on the torture of the mind to lie   21
In restless ecstasy. Duncan is in his grave;   22
After life's fitful fever he sleeps well.
Treason has done his worst: nor steel nor poison,
Malice domestic, foreign levy, nothing,   25
Can touch him further.

LADY   Come on.
Gentle my lord, sleek o'er your rugged looks;
Be bright and jovial among your guests to-night.

MACBETH
So shall I, love; and so, I pray, be you.
Let your remembrance apply to Banquo;   30
Present him eminence both with eye and tongue: 31
Unsafe the while, that we must lave   32
Our honors in these flattering streams
And make our faces vizards to our hearts,   34
Disguising what they are.

LADY   You must leave this.

MACBETH
O, full of scorpions is my mind, dear wife!
Thou know'st that Banquo, and his Fleance, lives.

LADY
But in them Nature's copy's not eterne.   38

MACBETH
There's comfort yet; they are assailable.
Then be thou jocund. Ere the bat hath flown
His cloistered flight, ere to black Hecate's summons
The shard-borne beetle with his drowsy hums   42
Hath rung night's yawning peal, there shall be done
A deed of dreadful note.

---

21 *torture* rack   22 *ecstasy* frenzy   25 *Malice domestic* civil war   30
remembrance i.e. awareness of the necessity   31 *Present him eminence*
exalt him   32 *lave* dip   34 *vizards* masks   38 *Nature's copy* Nature's
copyhold, lease on life   42 *shard-borne* borne on scaly wings

LADY   What's to be done?
MACBETH
     Be innocent of the knowledge, dearest chuck,
46 Till thou applaud the deed. Come, seeling night,
47 Scarf up the tender eye of pitiful day,
     And with thy bloody and invisible hand
49 Cancel and tear to pieces that great bond
     Which keeps me pale. Light thickens, and the crow
51 Makes wing to th' rooky wood.
     Good things of day begin to droop and drowse,
     Whiles night's black agents to their preys do rouse.
     Thou marvell'st at my words, but hold thee still;
     Things bad begun make strong themselves by ill.
     So prithee go with me.   *Exeunt.*

*

III, iii   *Enter three Murderers.*

1 . MURDERER
     But who did bid thee join with us?
3 . MURDERER   Macbeth.
2 . MURDERER
2 He needs not our mistrust, since he delivers
3 Our offices and what we have to do
     To the direction just.
1 . MURDERER   Then stand with us.
     The west yet glimmers with some streaks of day.
6 Now spurs the lated traveller apace
     To gain the timely inn, and near approaches
     The subject of our watch.
3 . MURDERER   Hark, I hear horses.

---

46 *seeling* sewing together the eyelids (from falconry) **47** *Scarf up* blindfold **49** *great bond* i.e. Banquo's lease on life (with suggestion also of the bond of human feeling) **51** *rooky* harboring rooks
III, iii An approach to the palace **2** *He needs not our mistrust* i.e. we need not mistrust this man **3** *offices* duties **6** *lated* belated

BANQUO *(within)*
    Give us a light there, ho!

2 . MURDERER   Then 'tis he : the rest
    That are within the note of expectation   10
    Already are i' th' court.

1 . MURDERER   His horses go about.

3 . MURDERER
    Almost a mile ; but he does usually,
    So all men do, from hence to th' palace gate
    Make it their walk.
        Enter Banquo and Fleance, with a torch.

2 . MURDERER
    A light, a light !

3 . MURDERER   'Tis he.

1 . MURDERER   Stand to't.

BANQUO
    It will be rain to-night.

1 . MURDERER   Let it come down !

BANQUO
    O, treachery ! Fly, good Fleance, fly, fly, fly !
        [Exit Fleance.]

    Thou mayst revenge – O slave !
    [Banquo slain.]

3 . MURDERER
    Who did strike out the light ?

1 . MURDERER   Was't not the way ?   19

3 . MURDERER
    There's but one down : the son is fled.

2 . MURDERER
    We have lost best half of our affair.

1 . MURDERER
    Well, let's away, and say how much is done.   *Exeunt*.

*

10 *within the note of expectation* on the list of those expected (invited) 19
Was't not the way i.e. was it not the right thing to do

67

III, iv   *Banquet prepared. Enter Macbeth, Lady [Macbeth],*
           Ross, Lennox, Lords, and Attendants.

MACBETH

1   You know your own degrees – sit down :
      At first and last the hearty welcome.

LORDS

      Thanks to your Majesty.

MACBETH

4   Ourself will mingle with society
      And play the humble host.

6   Our hostess keeps her state, but in best time
      We will require her welcome.

LADY

      Pronounce it for me, sir, to all our friends,
      For my heart speaks they are welcome.
             Enter First Murderer.

MACBETH

10   See, they encounter thee with their hearts' thanks.
      Both sides are even. Here I'll sit i' th' midst.
      Be large in mirth ; anon we'll drink a measure
      The table round.
             [Goes to Murderer.]
      There's blood upon thy face.

MURDERER   'Tis Banquo's then.

MACBETH

      'Tis better thee without than he within.
      Is he dispatched ?

MURDERER   My lord, his throat is cut :
      That I did for him.

MACBETH   Thou are the best o' th' cut-throats.
      Yet he's good that did the like for Fleance :
      If thou didst it, thou art the nonpareil.

MURDERER

      Most royal sir, Fleance is 'scaped.

III, iv The hall of the palace   1 *degrees* relative rank, order of precedence
4 *society* the company   6 *keeps her state* remains seated in her chair of state
10 *encounter* greet

MACBETH *[aside]*

    Then comes my fit again. I had else been perfect;   21

    Whole as the marble, founded as the rock,   22

    As broad and general as the casing air.   23

    But now I am cabined, cribbed, confined, bound in   24

    To saucy doubts and fears. – But Banquo's safe?   25

MURDERER

    Ay, my good lord. Safe in a ditch he bides,

    With twenty trenchèd gashes on his head,   27

    The least a death to nature.

MACBETH   Thanks for that. –

    [Aside]

    There the grown serpent lies; the worm that's fled   29

    Hath nature that in time will venom breed,

    No teeth for th' present. – Get thee gone. To-morrow

    We'll hear ourselves again.   *Exit Murderer.* 32

LADY   My royal lord,

    You do not give the cheer. The feast is sold   33

    That is not often vouched, while 'tis a-making,   34

    'Tis given with welcome. To feed were best at home;   35

    From thence, the sauce to meat is ceremony: 36

    Meeting were bare without it.   37

    Enter the Ghost of Banquo, and sits in Macbeth's

    place.

MACBETH   Sweet remembrancer!

    Now good digestion wait on appetite,

    And health on both!

LENNOX   May't please your Highness sit.

MACBETH

    Here had we now our country's honor roofed

    Were the graced person of our Banquo present –

---

21 *perfect* sound of health 22 *founded* solidly based 23 *broad and general* unconfined; *casing* enveloping 24 *cribbed* boxed in 25 *saucy* insolent 27 *trenchèd* deep, trench-like 29 *worm* serpent 32 *hear ourselves* confer 33 *cheer* tokens of convivial hospitality; *sold* i.e. not freely given 34 *vouched* sworn 35 *To feed . . . home* i.e. mere eating is best done at home 36 *meat* food 37 *bare* barren, pointless; *remembrancer* prompter

42   Who may I rather challenge for unkindness
    Than pity for mischance!

ROSS   His absence, sir.
    Lays blame upon his promise. Please't your Highness
    To grace us with your royal company?

MACBETH
    The table's full.

LENNOX   Here is a place reserved, sir.

MACBETH
    Where?

LENNOX
    Here, my good lord. What is't that moves your
        Highness?

MACBETH
    Which of you have done this?

LORDS   What, my good lord?

MACBETH
    Thou canst not say I did it. Never shake
    Thy gory locks at me.

ROSS
    Gentlemen, rise. His Highness is not well.

LADY
    Sit, worthy friends. My lord is often thus,
    And hath been from his youth. Pray you keep seat.
    The fit is momentary; upon a thought
    He will again be well. If much you note him,
57   You shall offend him and extend his passion.
    Feed, and regard him not. – Are you a man?

MACBETH
    Ay, and a bold one, that dare look on that
    Which might appal the devil.

LADY   O proper stuff!
    This is the very painting of your fear.
62   This is the air-drawn dagger which you said
63   Led you to Duncan. O, these flaws and starts

42 *Who may . . . challenge* whom I hope I may reprove   **57** *extend his passion*
prolong his seizure   **62** *air-drawn* fashioned of air   **63** *flaws* outbursts

(Impostors to true fear) would well become   64
A woman's story at a winter's fire,
Authorized by her grandam. Shame itself!   66
Why do you make such faces? When all's done,
You look but on a stool.

MACBETH   Prithee see there!
Behold! Look! Lo! – How say you?
Why, what care I? If thou canst nod, speak too.
If charnel houses and our graves must send
Those that we bury back, our monuments   72
Shall be the maws of kites.   *[Exit Ghost.]*   73

LADY   What, quite unmanned in folly?

MACBETH
If I stand here, I saw him.

LADY   Fie, for shame!

MACBETH
Blood hath been shed ere now, i' th' olden time,
Ere humane statute purged the gentle weal;   76
Ay, and since too, murders have been performed
Too terrible for the ear. The time has been
That, when the brains were out, the man would die,
And there an end. But now they rise again,
With twenty mortal murders on their crowns,   81
And push us from our stools. This is more strange
Than such a murder is.

LADY   My worthy lord,
Your noble friends do lack you.

MACBETH   I do forget.
Do not muse at me, my most worthy friends:
I have a strange infirmity, which is nothing
To those that know me. Come, love and health to all!
Then I'll sit down. Give me some wine, fill full.

---

64 *Impostors to true fear* (i.e. because they are authentic signs of false or
unjustified fear) **66** *Authorized* sanctioned **72** *monuments* i.e. our only
tombs **73** *maws of kites* bellies of ravens **76** *purged the gentle weal* i.e.
purged the state of savagery **81** *murders on their crowns* murderous
gashes on their heads

Enter Ghost.

I drink to th' general joy o' th' whole table,
And to our dear friend Banquo, whom we miss.

91   Would he were here ! To all, and him, we thirst,
92   And all to all.

LORDS   Our duties, and the pledge.

MACBETH

Avaunt, and quit my sight ! Let the earth hide thee !
Thy bones are marrowless, thy blood is cold ;

95   Thou hast no speculation in those eyes
Which thou dost glare with !

LADY   Think of this, good peers,
But as a thing of custom. 'Tis no other.
Only it spoils the pleasure of the time.

MACBETH

What man dare, I dare.
Approach thou like the rugged Russian bear,

101   The armed rhinoceros, or th' Hyrcan tiger ;
Take any shape but that, and my firm nerves
Shall never tremble. Or be alive again

104   And dare me to the desert with thy sword.
105   If trembling I inhabit then, protest me
106   The baby of a girl. Hence, horrible shadow !
Unreal mock'ry, hence !   *[Exit Ghost.]*

                     Why, so ; being gone,
I am a man again. Pray you sit still.

LADY

You have displaced the mirth, broke the good meeting

110   With most admired disorder.

MACBETH   Can such things be,

111   And overcome us like a summer's cloud

---

91 *thirst* are eager to drink   92 *all to all* let everyone drink to everyone
95 *speculation* intelligence, power of rational observation   101 *Hyrcan*
from Hyrcania, anciently a region near the Caspian Sea   104 *the desert*
a solitary place   105 *If trembling I inhabit* if I tremble   106 *The baby*
of a girl a baby girl   110 *admired* wondered at   111 *overcome us* come over
us

Without our special wonder? You make me strange   112
Even to the disposition that I owe,
When now I think you can behold such sights
And keep the natural ruby of your cheeks
When mine is blanched with fear.   116

ROSS   What sights, my lord?

LADY
I pray you speak not: he grows worse and worse;
Question enrages him. At once, good night.
Stand not upon the order of your going,
But go at once.

LENNOX   Good night and better health
Attend his Majesty.

LADY   A kind good night to all. *Exeunt Lords.*

MACBETH
It will have blood, they say: blood will have blood.
Stones have been known to move and trees to speak;
Augures and understood relations have   124
By maggot-pies and choughs and rooks brought forth   125
The secret'st man of blood. What is the night?

LADY
Almost at odds with morning, which is which.

MACBETH
How say'st thou, that Macduff denies his person
At our great bidding?

LADY   Did you send to him, sir?

MACBETH
I hear it by the way; but I will send.   130
There's not a one of them but in his house
I keep a servant fee'd. I will to-morrow   132
(And betimes I will) to the weird sisters.   133
More shall they speak, for now I am bent to know   134

112–13 *You make . . . I owe* you oust me from my proper role (as a brave
man)   116 *blanched* made pale   124 *Augures* auguries; *relations* utterances
125 *maggot-pies* magpies; *choughs* jackdaws (capable of 'utterances,' as are
magpies and rooks)   130 *by the way* casually   132 *fee'd* paid to spy   133
betimes speedily   134 *bent* inclined, determined

By the worst means the worst. For mine own good
All causes shall give way. I am in blood
Stepped in so far that, should I wade no more,
Returning were as tedious as go o'er.
Strange things I have in head, that will to hand,
140   Which must be acted ere they may be scanned.

LADY

141   You lack the season of all natures, sleep.

MACBETH

142   Come, we'll to sleep. My strange and self-abuse
143   Is the initiate fear that wants hard use.
We are yet but young in deed.   *Exeunt.*

*

III, v   [*Thunder. Enter the three Witches, meeting Hecate.*

1. WITCH

Why, how now, Hecate? You look angerly.

HECATE

2   Have I not reason, beldams as you are,
Saucy and overbold? How did you dare
To trade and traffic with Macbeth
In riddles and affairs of death;
And I, the mistress of your charms,
7   The close contriver of all harms,
Was never called to bear my part
Or show the glory of our art?
And, which is worse, all you have done
Hath been but for a wayward son,
Spiteful and wrathful, who, as others do,
Loves for his own ends, not for you.
But make amends now: get you gone

---

140 *ere they may be scanned* i.e. without being closely studied   141 *season*
seasoning, preservative   142 *self-abuse* delusion   143 *initiate fear* begin-
ner's fear; *wants hard use* lacks toughening practice
III, v An open place (an interpolated scene, by a different author)   2
beldams old crones   7 *close* secret

And at the pit of Acheron   15
Meet me i' th' morning. Thither he
Will come to know his destiny.
Your vessels and your spells provide,
Your charms and everything beside.
I am for th' air. This night I'll spend
Unto a dismal and a fatal end.
Great business must be wrought ere noon.
Upon the corner of the moon
There hangs a vap'rous drop profound;   24
I'll catch it ere it come to ground:
And that, distilled by magic sleights,   26
Shall raise such artificial sprites   27
As by the strength of their illusion
Shall draw him on to his confusion.
He shall spurn fate, scorn death, and bear
His hopes 'bove wisdom, grace, and fear:
And you all know security   32
Is mortals' chiefest enemy.
  Music, and a song.
Hark! I am called. My little spirit, see,
Sits in a foggy cloud and stays for me.   *[Exit.]*
  Sing within, 'Come away, come away,' &c.

1. WITCH
Come, let's make haste: she'll soon be back again.
          Exeunt.]

         ＊

Enter Lennox and another Lord.   III, vi

LENNOX
My former speeches have but hit your thoughts,   1
Which can interpret farther. Only I say   2
Things have been strangely borne. The gracious Duncan

15 *Acheron* a river of Hades 24 *profound* weighty 26 *sleights* devices 27
artificial sprites spirits created by magic arts 32 *security* over-confidence
III, vi Any meeting place in Scotland 1 *My former speeches* what I have
just said; *hit* matched 2 *interpret farther* draw further conclusions

Was pitied of Macbeth. Marry, he was dead.
And the right valiant Banquo walked too late;
Whom, you may say (if't please you) Fleance killed,
For Fleance fled. Men must not walk too late.
8 Who cannot want the thought how monstrous
It was for Malcolm and for Donalbain
10 To kill their gracious father? Damnèd fact,
How it did grieve Macbeth! Did he not straight,
In pious rage, the two delinquents tear
13 That were the slaves of drink and thralls of sleep?
Was not that nobly done? Ay, and wisely too,
For 'twould have angered any heart alive
To hear the men deny't. So that I say
17 He has borne all things well; and I do think
That, had he Duncan's sons under his key
19 (As, an't please heaven, he shall not), they should find
What 'twere to kill a father. So should Fleance.
21 But peace! for from broad words, and 'cause he failed
His presence at the tyrant's feast, I hear
Macduff lives in disgrace. Sir, can you tell
Where he bestows himself?

LORD   The son of Duncan,
25 From whom this tyrant holds the due of birth,
Lives in the English court, and is received
Of the most pious Edward with such grace
That the malevolence of fortune nothing
29 Takes from his high respect. Thither Macduff
30 Is gone to pray the holy King upon his aid
31 To wake Northumberland and warlike Siward;
That by the help of these (with Him above
To ratify the work) we may again
Give to our tables meat, sleep to our nights,

---

8 *cannot want the thought* can avoid thinking   10 *fact* deed   13 *thralls*
slaves   17 *borne* carried off   19 *an't* if it   21 *from broad words* through
plain speaking   25 *due of birth* birthright   29 *his high respect* high respect
for him   30 *upon his aid* upon Malcolm's behalf   31 *wake* arouse; *Northumberland* (English county bordering Scotland)

Free from our feasts and banquets bloody knives,
Do faithful homage and receive free honors –   36
All which we pine for now. And this report
Hath so exasperate the King that he
Prepares for some attempt of war.

LENNOX   Sent he to Macduff?

LORD
He did; and with an absolute 'Sir, not I,'
The cloudy messenger turns me his back   41
And hums, as who should say, 'You'll rue the time
That clogs me with this answer.'   43

LENNOX   And that well might
Advise him to a caution t' hold what distance   44
His wisdom can provide. Some holy angel
Fly to the court of England and unfold
His message ere he come, that a swift blessing
May soon return to this our suffering country
Under a hand accursed!

LORD   I'll send my prayers with him.
                                                Exeunt.

                          *

Thunder. Enter the three Witches.   IV, i
1. WITCH Thrice the brinded cat hath mewed.   1
2. WITCH Thrice, and once the hedge-pig whined.
3. WITCH Harpier cries. – 'Tis time, 'tis time!   3
1. WITCH Round about the cauldron go;
          In the poisoned entrails throw.
          Toad, that under cold stone
          Days and nights has thirty-one
          Swelt'red venom, sleeping got,   8
          Boil thou first i' th' charmèd pot.

---

36 *free* untainted   41 *cloudy* angry   43 *clogs* encumbers   44–45 *Advise him . . . can provide* warn him to keep at as safe a distance as he can devise   IV, i A cave (cf. III, v, 15)   1 *brinded* brindled, striped   3 *Harpier* (name of familiar spirit, suggestive of harpy)   8 *Swelt'red venom, sleeping got* exuded venom formed while sleeping

ALL   Double, double, toil and trouble,
                    Fire burn and cauldron bubble.

12 2. WITCH Fillet of a fenny snake,
                    In the cauldron boil and bake;
                    Eye of newt, and toe of frog,
                    Wool of bat, and tongue of dog,
16   Adder's fork, and blindworm's sting,
                    Lizard's leg, and howlet's wing –
                    For a charm of pow'rful trouble
                    Like a hell-broth boil and bubble.

ALL   Double, double, toil and trouble,
                    Fire burn and cauldron bubble.

    3. WITCH Scale of dragon, tooth of wolf,
23   Witch's mummy, maw and gulf
24   Of the ravined salt-sea shark,
                    Root of hemlock digged i' th' dark,
                    Liver of blaspheming Jew,
                    Gall of goat, and slips of yew
                    Slivered in the moon's eclipse,
                    Nose of Turk, and Tartar's lips,
                    Finger of birth-strangled babe
31   Ditch-delivered by a drab
32   Make the gruel thick and slab.
33   Add thereto a tiger's chaudron
                    For th' ingredience of our cauldron.

ALL   Double, double, toil and trouble,
                    Fire burn and cauldron bubble.

    2. WITCH Cool it with a baboon's blood,
38   Then the charm is firm and good.

                  [*Enter Hecate and the other three Witches*.

HECATE   O, well done! I commend your pains,
                    And every one shall share i' th' gains.
                    And now about the cauldron sing

---

12 *fenny* swamp 16 *blindworm* a lizard, popularly supposed poisonous 23 *mummy* mummified flesh; *maw and gulf* stomach and gullet 24 *ravined* insatiable 31 *drab* harlot 32 *slab* sticky 33 *chaudron* guts 38 s.d.–43 s.d. (an interpolation)

Like elves and fairies in a ring,
Enchanting all that you put in.
Music and a song, ' *Black spirits,*' *&c.*]
[*Exeunt Hecate and singers.*]

2. WITCH By the pricking of my thumbs,   44
Something wicked this way comes.
Open locks,
Whoever knocks!
Enter Macbeth.

MACBETH
How now, you secret, black, and midnight hags,
What is't you do?

ALL   A deed without a name.

MACBETH
I conjure you by that which you profess,
Howe'er you come to know it, answer me.
Though you untie the winds and let them fight
Against the churches, though the yesty waves   53
Confound and swallow navigation up,   54
Though bladed corn be lodged and trees blown down,   55
Though castles topple on their warders' heads,
Though palaces and pyramids do slope   57
Their heads to their foundations, though the treasure
Of Nature's germains tumble all together   59
Even till destruction sicken, answer me   60
To what I ask you.

1. WITCH   Speak.
2. WITCH   Demand.
3. WITCH   We'll answer.
1. WITCH
Say if th' hadst rather hear it from our mouths
Or from our masters.

MACBETH   Call 'em. Let me see 'em.

1. WITCH Pour in sow's blood, that hath eaten

---

44 *By* i.e. I know by **53** *yesty* yeasty, foamy **54** *Confound* destroy **55**
bladed corn be lodged ripe grain be beaten to earth **57** *slope* incline **59**
Nature's germains seeds of creation **60** *sicken* shall surfeit

65   Her nine farrow; grease that's sweaten
             From the murderer's gibbet throw
             Into the flame.

ALL   Come, high or low,
68   Thyself and office deftly show!

Thunder. First Apparition, an Armed Head.

MACBETH
    Tell me, thou unknown power –

1. WITCH   He knows thy thought:
    Hear his speech, but say thou naught.

1. APPARITION
    Macbeth, Macbeth, Macbeth, beware Macduff!
    Beware the Thane of Fife! Dismiss me. – Enough.

                               He descends.

MACBETH
    Whate'er thou art, for thy good caution thanks:
74   Thou hast harped my fear aright. But one word more –

1. WITCH
    He will not be commanded. Here's another,
    More potent than the first.

        Thunder. Second Apparition, a Bloody Child.

2. APPARITION
    Macbeth, Macbeth, Macbeth –

MACBETH
    Had I three ears, I'ld hear thee.

2. APPARITION
    Be bloody, bold, and resolute! Laugh to scorn
    The pow'r of man, for none of woman born
    Shall harm Macbeth.   *Descends.*

MACBETH
    Then live, Macduff, – what need I fear of thee?
    But yet I'll make assurance double sure
84   And take a bond of fate. Thou shalt not live;
    That I may tell pale-hearted fear it lies
    And sleep in spite of thunder.

---

65 *nine farrow* litter of nine   68 *office* function   74 *harped* hit the tune of
84 *take a bond of* secure a guarantee from

*Thunder. Third Apparition, a Child Crowned, with
a tree in his hand.*

                              What is this
That rises like the issue of a king
And wears upon his baby-brow the round   88
And top of sovereignty?

ALL   Listen, but speak not to't.

3. APPARITION
Be lion-mettled, proud, and take no care
Who chafes, who frets, or where conspirers are!
Macbeth shall never vanquished be until
Great Birnam Wood to high Dunsinane Hill
Shall come against him.   *Descends.*

MACBETH   That will never be.
Who can impress the forest, bid the tree   95
Unfix his earth-bound root? Sweet bodements, good!   96
Rebellious dead rise never till the Wood
Of Birnam rise, and our high-placed Macbeth
Shall live the lease of nature, pay his breath   99
To time and mortal custom. Yet my heart   100
Throbs to know one thing. Tell me, if your art
Can tell so much: Shall Banquo's issue ever   102
Reign in this kingdom?

ALL   Seek to know no more.

MACBETH
I will be satisfied. Deny me this,
And an eternal curse fall on you! Let me know.
Why sinks that cauldron? and what noise is this?   106
          Hautboys.

1. WITCH Show!
2. WITCH Show!
3. WITCH Show!
ALL   Show his eyes, and grieve his heart!
          Come like shadows, so depart!

---

88 *round* crown   95 *impress* conscript   96 *bodements* prophecies   99 *lease
of nature* i.e. the full life-span   100 *mortal custom* normal death   102 *issue*
offspring   106 *noise* music

A show of eight Kings and Banquo, last [King] with a glass in his hand.

MACBETH
Thou art too like the spirit of Banquo. Down!
Thy crown does sear mine eyeballs. And thy hair,
Thou other gold-bound brow, is like the first.
A third is like the former. Filthy hags,
116   Why do you show me this? A fourth? Start, eyes!
What, will the line stretch out to th' crack of doom?
Another yet? A seventh? I'll see no more.
And yet the eighth appears, who bears a glass
Which shows me many more; and some I see
121   That twofold balls and treble sceptres carry.
Horrible sight! Now I see 'tis true;
123   For the blood-boltered Banquo smiles upon me
And points at them for his. What? Is this so?
125   [1. WITCH   Ay, sir, all this is so. But why
                      Stands Macbeth thus amazedly?
127   Come, sisters, cheer we up his sprites
                      And show the best of our delights.
                      I'll charm the air to give a sound
130   While you perform your antic round,
                      That this great king may kindly say
                      Our duties did his welcome pay.
                          Music. The Witches dance, and vanish.]

MACBETH
Where are they? Gone? Let this pernicious hour
Stand aye accursèd in the calendar!
Come in, without there!
        Enter Lennox.
LENNOX   What's your Grace's will?
MACBETH
Saw you the weird sisters?
LENNOX   No, my lord.

116 *Start* bulge   121 *twofold balls and treble sceptres* (English coronation insignia)   123 *blood-boltered* matted with blood   125–32 (an interpolation) 127 *sprites* spirits   130 *antic round* grotesque circular dance

MACBETH
    Came they not by you?
LENNOX   No indeed, my lord.
MACBETH
    Infected be the air whereon they ride,
    And damned all those that trust them! I did hear
    The galloping of horse. Who was't came by?
LENNOX
    'Tis two or three, my lord, that bring you word
    Macduff is fled to England.
MACBETH   Fled to England?
LENNOX
    Ay, my good lord.
MACBETH [aside]
    Time, thou anticipat'st my dread exploits.   144
    The flighty purpose never is o'ertook   145
    Unless the deed go with it. From this moment
    The very firstlings of my heart shall be   147
    The firstlings of my hand. And even now,
    To crown my thoughts with acts, be it thought and done:
    The castle of Macduff I will surprise,
    Seize upon Fife, give to th' edge o' th' sword
    His wife, his babes, and all unfortunate souls
    That trace him in his line. No boasting like a fool;   153
    This deed I'll do before this purpose cool.
    But no more sights! – Where are these gentlemen?
    Come, bring me where they are.   *Exeunt.*

                          *

            Enter Macduff's Wife, her Son, and Ross.   IV, ii
WIFE
    What had he done to make him fly the land?

144 *anticipat'st* forestall   145 *flighty* fleeting   147–48 *firstlings . . . my hand*
i.e. I shall act at the moment I feel the first impulse   153 *trace* follow; *line*
family line
IV, ii Within the castle at Fife

ROSS
2 You must have patience, madam.
WIFE   He had none.
   His flight was madness. When our actions do not,
4 Our fears do make us traitors.
ROSS   You know not
   Whether it was his wisdom or his fear.
WIFE
   Wisdom? To leave his wife, to leave his babes,
   His mansion and his titles in a place
   From whence himself does fly? He loves us not,
9 He wants the natural touch. For the poor wren
   (The most diminutive of birds) will fight,
   Her young ones in her nest, against the owl.
   All is the fear and nothing is the love,
   As little is the wisdom, where the flight
   So runs against all reason.
14 ROSS   My dearest coz,
   I pray you school yourself. But for your husband,
   He is noble, wise, judicious, and best knows
17 The fits o' th' season. I dare not speak much further,
   But cruel are the times when we are traitors
19 And do not know ourselves; when we hold rumor
   From what we fear, yet know not what we fear
   But float upon a wild and violent sea
   Each way and none. I take my leave of you.
   Shall not be long but I'll be here again.
24 Things at the worst will cease, or else climb upward
   To what they were before. – My pretty cousin,
   Blessing upon you!
WIFE
   Fathered he is, and yet he's fatherless.

2 *patience* self-control   4 *traitors* i.e. traitors to ourselves   9 *wants* lacks
14 *coz* cousin, kinswoman   17 *fits o' th' season* present disorders   19
know ourselves know ourselves to be so   19–20 *hold rumor . . . we fear*
are credulous in accordance with our fears   24 *will cease* i.e. must cease
descending

ROSS
   I am so much a fool, should I stay longer
   It would be my disgrace and your discomfort.   29
   I take my leave at once.   *Exit.*
WIFE   Sirrah, your father's dead;
   And what will you do now? How will you live?
SON
   As birds do, mother.
WIFE   What, with worms and flies?
SON
   With what I get, I mean; and so do they.
WIFE
   Poor bird! thou'dst never fear the net nor lime,   34
   The pitfall nor the gin.   35
SON
   Why should I, mother? Poor birds they are not set for.
   My father is not dead for all your saying.
WIFE
   Yes, he is dead. How wilt thou do for a father?
SON Nay, how will you do for a husband?
WIFE Why, I can buy me twenty at any market.
SON Then you'll buy 'em to sell again.   41
WIFE
   Thou speak'st with all thy wit; and yet, i' faith,   42
   With wit enough for thee.
SON
   Was my father a traitor, mother?
WIFE Ay, that he was!
SON What is a traitor?
WIFE Why, one that swears and lies.
SON And be all traitors that do so?
WIFE Every one that does so is a traitor and must be
   hanged.
SON And must they all be hanged that swear and lie?

29 *would be my* would be to my (i.e. his weeping)   34 *lime* birdlime   35
gin trap   41 *sell* betray   42–43 *Thou speak'st . . . for thee* i.e. you use all the
intelligence you have, and it is quite enough

WIFE Every one.

SON Who must hang them?

WIFE Why, the honest men.

SON Then the liars and swearers are fools, for there are
56   liars and swearers enow to beat the honest men and
hang up them.

WIFE Now God help thee, poor monkey! But how wilt
thou do for a father?

SON If he were dead, you'ld weep for him. If you would
not, it were a good sign that I should quickly have a new
father.

WIFE Poor prattler, how thou talk'st!
Enter a Messenger.

MESSENGER
Bless you, fair dame! I am not to you known,
65   Though in your state of honor I am perfect.
66   I doubt some danger does approach you nearly.
67   If you will take a homely man's advice,
Be not found here. Hence with your little ones!
To fright you thus methinks I am too savage;
70   To do worse to you were fell cruelty,
Which is too nigh your person. Heaven preserve you!
I dare abide no longer.   *Exit.*

WIFE   Whither should I fly?
I have done no harm. But I remember now
I am in this earthly world, where to do harm
Is often laudable, to do good sometime
Accounted dangerous folly. Why then, alas,
Do I put up that womanly defense
To say I have done no harm?
Enter Murderers.   What are these faces?

MURDERER
Where is your husband?

56 *enow* enough **65** *in your state . . . perfect* I am informed of your noble
identity **66** *doubt* fear **67** *homely* plain **70–71** *To do worse . . . your
person* i.e. not to frighten you were to do worse, expose you to that fierce
cruelty which is impending

WIFE
    I hope in no place so unsanctified
    Where such as thou mayst find him.
MURDERER   He's a traitor.
SON
    Thou liest, thou shag-eared villain !   82
MURDERER   What, you egg !
    [Stabs him.]
    Young fry of treachery !   83
SON   He has killed me, mother.
    Run away, I pray you !
    [Dies.]   Exit [Wife], crying 'Murder !'
                      [pursued by Murderers].

                    *

    Enter Malcolm and Macduff.   IV, iii
MALCOLM
    Let us seek out some desolate shade, and there
    Weep our sad bosoms empty.
MACDUFF   Let us rather
    Hold fast the mortal sword and, like good men,   3
    Bestride our downfall'n birthdom. Each new morn   4
    New widows howl, new orphans cry, new sorrows
    Strike heaven on the face, that it resounds
    As if it felt with Scotland and yelled out
    Like syllable of dolor.   8
MALCOLM   What I believe, I'll wail ;
    What know, believe ; and what I can redress,
    As I shall find the time to friend, I will.   10
    What you have spoke, it may be so perchance.
    This tyrant, whose sole name blisters our tongues,   12
    Was once thought honest ; you have loved him well ;

---

82 shag-eared i.e. with shaggy hair falling about the ears   83 fry spawn
IV, iii The grounds of the King's palace in England   3 mortal deadly
4 Bestride i.e. stand over protectively; birthdom place of birth   8 Like
syllable of dolor a similar cry of pain   10 time to friend time propitious
12 sole name very name

14   He hath not touched you yet. I am young ; but something
15   You may deserve of him through me, and wisdom
      To offer up a weak, poor, innocent lamb
      T' appease an angry god.

MACDUFF
  I am not treacherous.

MALCOLM   But Macbeth is.

19   A good and virtuous nature may recoil
      In an imperial charge. But I shall crave your pardon.
21   That which you are, my thoughts cannot transpose :
22   Angels are bright still though the brightest fell ;
      Though all things foul would wear the brows of grace,
      Yet grace must still look so.

MACDUFF   I have lost my hopes.

MALCOLM
  Perchance even there where I did find my doubts.
26   Why in that rawness left you wife and child,
      Those precious motives, those strong knots of love,
      Without leave-taking ? I pray you,
29   Let not my jealousies be your dishonors,
      But mine own safeties. You may be rightly just
      Whatever I shall think.

MACDUFF   Bleed, bleed, poor country !
32   Great tyranny, lay thou thy basis sure,
      For goodness dare not check thee ; wear thou thy wrongs,
34   The title is affeered ! Fare thee well, lord.
      I would not be the villain that thou think'st
      For the whole space that's in the tyrant's grasp
      And the rich East to boot.

MALCOLM   Be not offended.
38   I speak not as in absolute fear of you.
      I think our country sinks beneath the yoke,

---

14 *young* i.e. young and inexperienced   15 *wisdom* i.e. it may be wise
19-20 *recoil . . . imperial charge* reverse itself under royal pressure   21
transpose alter   22 *the brightest* i.e. Lucifer   26 *rawness* unprotected state
29 *jealousies* suspicions   32 *basis* foundation   34 *affeered* confirmed by law
38 *absolute* complete

It weeps, it bleeds, and each new day a gash
Is added to her wounds. I think withal   41
There would be hands uplifted in my right;
And here from gracious England have I offer
Of goodly thousands. But, for all this,
When I shall tread upon the tyrant's head
Or wear it on my sword, yet my poor country
Shall have more vices than it had before,
More suffer, and more sundry ways than ever,
By him that shall succeed.

MACDUFF   What should he be?

MALCOLM
It is myself I mean, in whom I know
All the particulars of vice so grafted   51
That, when they shall be opened, black Macbeth   52
Will seem as pure as snow, and the poor state
Esteem him as a lamb, being compared
With my confineless harms.   55

MACDUFF   Not in the legions
Of horrid hell can come a devil more damned
In evils to top Macbeth.

MALCOLM   I grant him bloody,
Luxurious, avaricious, false, deceitful,   58
Sudden, malicious, smacking of every sin   59
That has a name. But there's no bottom, none,
In my voluptuousness. Your wives, your daughters,
Your matrons, and your maids could not fill up
The cistern of my lust; and my desire
All continent impediments would o'erbear   64
That did oppose my will. Better Macbeth
Than such an one to reign.

MACDUFF   Boundless intemperance
In nature is a tyranny. It hath been   67

41 *withal* furthermore   51 *particulars* varieties; *grafted* implanted   52
opened revealed   55 *confineless harms* unlimited vices   58 *Luxurious*
lecherous   59 *Sudden* violent   64 *continent* containing, restraining   67
In nature in one's nature

Th' untimely emptying of the happy throne
And fall of many kings. But fear not yet
To take upon you what is yours. You may
71   Convey your pleasures in a spacious plenty
And yet seem cold – the time you may so hoodwink.
We have willing dames enough. There cannot be
That vulture in you to devour so many
As will to greatness dedicate themselves,
Finding it so inclined.

MALCOLM   With this there grows
77   In my most ill-composed affection such
78   A stanchless avarice that, were I King,
I should cut off the nobles for their lands,
Desire his jewels, and this other's house,
And my more-having would be as a sauce
82   To make me hunger more, that I should forge
Quarrels unjust against the good and loyal,
Destroying them for wealth.

MACDUFF   This avarice
Sticks deeper, grows with more pernicious root
86   Than summer-seeming lust, and it hath been
87   The sword of our slain kings. Yet do not fear.
88   Scotland hath foisons to fill up your will
89   Of your mere own. All these are portable,
With other graces weighed.

MALCOLM
But I have none. The king-becoming graces,
As justice, verity, temp'rance, stableness,
93   Bounty, perseverance, mercy, lowliness,
Devotion, patience, courage, fortitude,
95   I have no relish of them, but abound
96   In the division of each several crime,

---

71 *Convey* obtain by stealth   77 *ill-composed affection* disordered disposition   78 *stanchless* insatiable   82 *forge* fabricate   86 *summer-seeming* i.e. seasonal, transitory   87 *sword of our slain* cause of death of our   88–89 *foisons . . . mere own* riches of your own enough to satisfy you   89 *portable* bearable   93 *lowliness* humility   95 *relish* trace   96 *division* subdivisions

Acting in many ways. Nay, had I pow'r, I should
Pour the sweet milk of concord into hell,
Uproar the universal peace, confound   99
All unity on earth.

MACDUFF   O Scotland, Scotland!

MALCOLM
If such a one be fit to govern, speak.
I am as I have spoken.

MACDUFF   Fit to govern?
No, not to live! O nation miserable,
With an untitled tyrant bloody-sceptred,
When shalt thou see thy wholesome days again,
Since that the truest issue of thy throne
By his own interdiction stands accursed   107
And does blaspheme his breed? Thy royal father
Was a most sainted king; the queen that bore thee,
Oft'ner upon her knees than on her feet,
Died every day she lived. Fare thee well.   111
These evils thou repeat'st upon thyself
Hath banished me from Scotland. O my breast,
Thy hope ends here!

MALCOLM   Macduff, this noble passion,
Child of integrity, hath from my soul
Wiped the black scruples, reconciled my thoughts   116
To thy good truth and honor. Devilish Macbeth
By many of these trains hath sought to win me   118
Into his power; and modest wisdom plucks me   119
From over-credulous haste; but God above
Deal between thee and me, for even now
I put myself to thy direction and
Unspeak mine own detraction, here abjure
The taints and blames I laid upon myself
For strangers to my nature. I am yet   125
Unknown to woman, never was forsworn,

99 *Uproar* blast 107 *interdiction* curse 111 *Died* i.e. turned away from
this life 116 *scruples* doubts 118 *trains* plots 119 *modest* cautious;
plucks holds 125 *For* as

Scarcely have coveted what was mine own,
At no time broke my faith, would not betray
The devil to his fellow, and delight
No less in truth than life. My first false speaking

131   Was this upon myself. What I am truly,
Is thine and my poor country's to command ;
Whither indeed, before thy here-approach,
Old Siward with ten thousand warlike men

135   Already at a point was setting forth.

136   Now we'll together ; and the chance of goodness
Be like our warranted quarrel ! Why are you silent ?

MACDUFF
Such welcome and unwelcome things at once
'Tis hard to reconcile.
          Enter a Doctor.

MALCOLM
140   Well, more anon. Comes the King forth, I pray you ?

DOCTOR
Ay, sir. There are a crew of wretched souls
142   That stay his cure. Their malady convinces
143   The great assay of art ; but at his touch,
Such sanctity hath heaven given his hand,
They presently amend.

MALCOLM   I thank you, doctor. *Exit [Doctor].*
MACDUFF
What's the disease he means ?

146   MALCOLM   'Tis called the evil.
A most miraculous work in this good King,
Which often since my here-remain in England
I have seen him do : how he solicits heaven

150   Himself best knows, but strangely-visited people,
All swol'n and ulcerous, pitiful to the eye,

---

131 *upon* against   135 *at a point* armed   136–37 *the chance . . . warranted quarrel* i.e. let the chance of success equal the justice of our cause   140 *anon* soon   142 *stay* await; *convinces* baffles   143 *assay of art* resources of medical science   146 *evil* scrofula (king's evil)   150 *strangely-visited* unusually afflicted

The mere despair of surgery, he cures,   152
Hanging a golden stamp about their necks,   153
Put on with holy prayers ; and 'tis spoken,
To the succeeding royalty he leaves
The healing benediction. With this strange virtue,
He hath a heavenly gift of prophecy,
And sundry blessings hang about his throne
That speak him full of grace.
  Enter Ross.

MACDUFF   See who comes here.
MALCOLM
 My countryman ; but yet I know him not.
MACDUFF
 My ever gentle cousin, welcome hither.
MALCOLM
 I know him now. Good God betimes remove   162
 The means that makes us strangers !
ROSS   Sir, amen.
MACDUFF
 Stands Scotland where it did ?
ROSS   Alas, poor country,
 Almost afraid to know itself. It cannot
 Be called our mother but our grave, where nothing   166
 But who knows nothing is once seen to smile ;
 Where signs and groans, and shrieks that rent the air,
 Are made, not marked ; where violent sorrow seems   169
 A modern ecstasy. The dead man's knell   170
 Is there scarce asked for who, and good men's lives   171
 Expire before the flowers in their caps,
 Dying or ere they sicken.
MACDUFF   O, relation   173
 Too nice, and yet too true !   174
MALCOLM   What's the newest grief ?

---

152 *mere* utter 153 *stamp* coin 162 *betimes* quickly 166 *nothing* no one
169 *marked* noticed 170 *modern ecstasy* commonplace emotion 171 *Is
there . . . for who* scarcely calls forth an inquiry about identity 173 *relation*
report 174 *nice* precise

ROSS

175   That of an hour's age doth hiss the speaker ;
176   Each minute teems a new one.

MACDUFF   How does my wife ?

ROSS

Why, well.

MACDUFF   And all my children ?

ROSS   Well too.

MACDUFF

The tyrant has not battered at their peace ?

ROSS

No, they were well at peace when I did leave 'em.

MACDUFF

Be not a niggard of your speech. How goes't ?

ROSS

When I came hither to transport the tidings
182   Which I have heavily borne, there ran a rumor
183   Of many worthy fellows that were out,
184   Which was to my belief witnessed the rather
For that I saw the tyrant's power afoot.
Now is the time of help. Your eye in Scotland
Would create soldiers, make our women fight
To doff their dire distresses.

MALCOLM   Be't their comfort
We are coming thither. Gracious England hath
Lent us good Siward and ten thousand men,
An older and a better soldier none
192   That Christendom gives out.

ROSS   Would I could answer
This comfort with the like. But I have words
That would be howled out in the desert air,
195   Where hearing should not latch them.

MACDUFF   What concern they,

175 *doth hiss the speaker* causes the speaker to be hissed (for stale repetition)
176 *teems* brings forth   182 *heavily borne* sadly carried   183 *out* up in
arms   184 *witnessed* attested   192 *gives out* reports   195 *latch* catch hold of

The general cause or is it a fee-grief   196
Due to some single breast?   197

ROSS   No mind that's honest
But in it shares some woe, though the main part
Pertains to you alone.

MACDUFF   If it be mine,
Keep it not from me; quickly let me have it.

ROSS
Let not your ears despise my tongue for ever,
Which shall possess them with the heaviest sound
That ever yet they heard.

MACDUFF   Humh! I guess at it.

ROSS
Your castle is surprised, your wife and babes   204
Savagely slaughtered. To relate the manner
Were, on the quarry of these murdered deer,   206
To add the death of you.

MALCOLM   Merciful heaven!
What, man! Ne'er pull your hat upon your brows.
Give sorrow words. The grief that does not speak   209
Whispers the o'erfraught heart and bids it break.   210

MACDUFF
My children too?

ROSS   Wife, children, servants, all
That could be found.

MACDUFF   And I must be from thence?
My wife killed too?

ROSS   I have said.

MALCOLM   Be comforted.
Let's make us med'cines of our great revenge
To cure this deadly grief.

MACDUFF
He has no children. All my pretty ones?

---

196 *fee-grief* i.e. a grief possessed in private   197 *Due* belonging   204
surprised attacked   206 *quarry* heap of game   209 *speak* speak aloud
210 *Whispers* whispers to

Did you say all? O hell-kite! All?
What, all my pretty chickens and their dam
At one fell swoop?

MALCOLM

220 Dispute it like a man.

MACDUFF   I shall do so;
But I must also feel it as a man.
I cannot but remember such things were
That were most precious to me. Did heaven look on
And would not take their part? Sinful Macduff,

225 They were all struck for thee! Naught that I am,
Not for their own demerits but for mine
Fell slaughter on their souls. Heaven rest them now!

MALCOLM

Be this the whetstone of your sword. Let grief
Convert to anger; blunt not the heart, enrage it.

MACDUFF

O, I could play the woman with mine eyes
And braggart with my tongue. But, gentle heavens,

232 Cut short all intermission. Front to front
Bring thou this fiend of Scotland and myself.
Within my sword's length set him. If he scape,
Heaven forgive him too!

MALCOLM   This tune goes manly.

236 Come, go we to the King. Our power is ready;
237 Our lack is nothing but our leave. Macbeth
Is ripe for shaking, and the pow'rs above
239 Put on their instruments. Receive what cheer you may.
The night is long that never finds the day.   *Exeunt.*

*

220 *Dispute* revenge   **225** *Naught* wicked   **232** *intermission* interval; *Front to front* face to face   **236** *power* army   **237** *Our lack ... our leave* i.e. nothing remains but to say farewell   **239** *Put on their instruments* urge on their agents

Enter a Doctor of Physic and a Waiting Gentlewoman. V, i

DOCTOR I have two nights watched with you, but can
perceive no truth in your report. When was it she last
walked?

GENTLEWOMAN Since his Majesty went into the field I
have seen her rise from her bed, throw her nightgown 5
upon her, unlock her closet, take forth paper, fold it, 6
write upon't, read it, afterwards seal it, and again return
to bed; yet all this while in a most fast sleep.

DOCTOR A great perturbation in nature, to receive at once
the benefit of sleep and do the effects of watching! In this 10
slumb'ry agitation, besides her walking and other actual
performances, what (at any time) have you heard her say?

GENTLEWOMAN That, sir, which I will not report after
her.

DOCTOR You may to me, and 'tis most meet you should. 14

GENTLEWOMAN Neither to you nor any one, having no
witness to confirm my speech.

Enter Lady [Macbeth], with a taper.

Lo you, here she comes! This is her very guise, and, 17
upon my life, fast asleep! Observe her; stand close. 18

DOCTOR How came she by that light?

GENTLEWOMAN Why, it stood by her. She has light by
her continually. 'Tis her command.

DOCTOR You see her eyes are open.

GENTLEWOMAN Ay, but their sense are shut. 23

DOCTOR What is it she does now? Look how she rubs her
hands.

GENTLEWOMAN It is an accustomed action with her, to
seem thus washing her hands. I have known her continue in this a quarter of an hour.

LADY Yet here's a spot.

DOCTOR Hark, she speaks. I will set down what comes

V, i Within Macbeth's castle at Dunsinane   5 *nightgown* dressing gown   6
closet a chest, or desk   10 *do the effects of watching* act as if awake   14 *meet*
fitting   17 *guise* habit   18 *close* concealed   23 *sense* powers of sensation

from her, to satisfy my remembrance the more strongly.

LADY Out, damned spot! Out, I say! One – two – why
then 'tis time to do't. Hell is murky. Fie, my lord, fie! a
soldier and afeard? What need we fear who knows it,
35   when none can call our power to accompt? Yet who
would have thought the old man to have had so much
blood in him?

DOCTOR Do you mark that?

LADY The Thane of Fife had a wife. Where is she now?
What, will these hands ne'er be clean? No more o' that,
my lord, no more o' that! You mar all with this
42   starting.

DOCTOR Go to, go to! You have known what you should
not.

GENTLEWOMAN She has spoke what she should not, I
am sure of that. Heaven knows what she has known.

LADY Here's the smell of the blood still. All the perfumes
of Arabia will not sweeten this little hand. Oh, oh, oh!

49 DOCTOR What a sigh is there! The heart is sorely charged.

GENTLEWOMAN I would not have such a heart in my
bosom for the dignity of the whole body.

DOCTOR Well, well, well.

GENTLEWOMAN Pray God it be, sir.

54 DOCTOR This disease is beyond my practice. Yet I have
known those which have walked in their sleep who have
died holily in their beds.

LADY Wash your hands, put on your nightgown, look
not so pale! I tell you yet again, Banquo 's buried. He
cannot come out on's grave.

DOCTOR Even so?

LADY To bed, to bed! There's knocking at the gate.
Come, come, come, come, give me your hand! What's
done cannot be undone. To bed, to bed, to bed!   *Exit.*

DOCTOR Will she go now to bed?

---

35 *call our power to accompt* call to account anyone so powerful as we   42
starting startled movements   49 *charged* laden   54 *practice* professional
competence

GENTLEWOMAN Directly.

DOCTOR
 Foul whisp'rings are abroad. Unnatural deeds
 Do breed unnatural troubles. Infected minds
 To their deaf pillows will discharge their secrets.
 More needs she the divine than the physician.
 God, God forgive us all ! Look after her ;
 Remove from her the means of all annoyance, 71
 And still keep eyes upon her. So good night.
 My mind she has mated, and amazed my sight. 73
 I think, but dare not speak.

GENTLEWOMAN   Good night, good doctor.

            Exeunt.

*

Drum and Colors. Enter Menteith, Caithness, V, ii
Angus, Lennox, Soldiers.

MENTEITH
 The English pow'r is near, led on by Malcolm,
 His uncle Siward, and the good Macduff.
 Revenges burn in them ; for their dear causes
 Would to the bleeding and the grim alarm 4
 Excite the mortified man. 5

ANGUS   Near Birnam Wood
 Shall we well meet them ; that way are they coming. 6

CAITHNESS
 Who knows if Donalbain be with his brother ?

LENNOX
 For certain, sir, he is not. I have a file 8
 Of all the gentry. There is Siward's son
 And many unrough youths that even now 10
 Protest their first of manhood. 11

MENTEITH   What does the tyrant ?

---

71 *annoyance* self-injury 73 *mated* bemused
V, ii Open country near Birnam Wood and Dunsinane 4 *bleeding* blood
of battle 5 *Excite* incite; *mortified* dead 6 *well* surely 8 *file* list 10
unrough unbearded 11 *Protest* assert

CAITHNESS
　　Great Dunsinane he strongly fortifies.
　　Some say he's mad; others, that lesser hate him,
　　Do call it valiant fury; but for certain
15　　He cannot buckle his distempered cause
16　　Within the belt of rule.

ANGUS　　　　　　　Now does he feel
　　His secret murders sticking on his hands.
18　　Now minutely revolts upbraid his faith-breach.
　　Those he commands move only in command,
　　Nothing in love. Now does he feel his title
　　Hang loose about him, like a giant's robe
　　Upon a dwarfish thief.

MENTEITH　　　　　　Who then shall blame
23　　His pestered senses to recoil and start,
　　When all that is within him does condemn
　　Itself for being there?

CAITHNESS　　　　　Well, march we on
　　To give obedience where 'tis truly owed.
27　　Meet we the med'cine of the sickly weal;
　　And with him pour we in our country's purge
　　Each drop of us.

LENNOX　　　　Or so much as it needs
30　　To dew the sovereign flower and drown the weeds.
　　Make we our march towards Birnam.　*Exeunt, marching.*

✳

V, iii　　　　　*Enter Macbeth, Doctor, and Attendants.*
MACBETH
　　Bring me no more reports. Let them fly all!
　　Till Birnam Wood remove to Dunsinane,

15 *distempered* disease-swollen　**16** *rule* reason　**18** *minutely* every minute;
revolts rebellions　**23** *pestered* tormented　**27** *med'cine* cure (i.e. Malcolm);
weal commonwealth　**30** *dew* water
V, iii Within Dunsinane Castle

I cannot taint with fear. What's the boy Malcolm?   3
Was he not born of woman? The spirits that know
All mortal consequences have pronounced me thus: 5
'Fear not, Macbeth. No man that's born of woman
Shall e'er have power upon thee.' Then fly, false thanes,
And mingle with the English epicures.   8
The mind I sway by and the heart I bear   9
Shall never sag with doubt nor shake with fear.
  Enter Servant.
The devil damn thee black, thou cream-faced loon!   11
Where got'st thou that goose look?

SERVANT
 There is ten thousand –

MACBETH   Geese, villain?

SERVANT   Soldiers, sir.

MACBETH
 Go prick thy face and over-red thy fear,   14
 Thou lily-livered boy. What soldiers, patch?   15
 Death of thy soul! those linen cheeks of thine
 Are counsellors to fear. What soldiers, whey-face?

SERVANT
 The English force, so please you.

MACBETH
 Take thy face hence.   *[Exit Servant.]*
     Seyton! – I am sick at heart,
When I behold – Seyton, I say! – This push   20
Will cheer me ever, or disseat me now.
I have lived long enough. My way of life
Is fall'n into the sear, the yellow leaf,   23
And that which should accompany old age,
As honor, love, obedience, troops of friends,
I must not look to have; but, in their stead,

---

3 *taint* become tainted **5** *consequences* sequence of events **8** *English epicures* (i.e. as compared with the austerely-living Scots) **9** *sway* direct myself **11** *loon* lout **14** *over-red thy fear* i.e. paint red over your fearful pallor **15** *patch* fool **20** *push* struggle **23** *sear* dry, withered

Curses not loud but deep, mouth-honor, breath,
Which the poor heart would fain deny, and dare not.
Seyton!

Enter Seyton.

SEYTON
What's your gracious pleasure?

MACBETH   What news more?

SEYTON
All is confirmed, my lord, which was reported.

MACBETH
I'll fight till from my bones my flesh be hacked.
Give me my armor.

SEYTON   'Tis not needed yet.

MACBETH
I'll put it on.

35 Send out moe horses, skirr the country round,
Hang those that talk of fear. Give me mine armor.
How does your patient, doctor?

DOCTOR   Not so sick, my lord,
As she is troubled with thick-coming fancies
That keep her from her rest.

MACBETH   Cure her of that!
Canst thou not minister to a mind diseased,
Pluck from the memory a rooted sorrow,

42 Raze out the written troubles of the brain,
43 And with some sweet oblivious antidote
44 Cleanse the stuffed bosom of that perilous stuff
Which weighs upon the heart?

DOCTOR   Therein the patient
Must minister to himself.

MACBETH
47 Throw physic to the dogs, I'll none of it!
Come, put mine armor on. Give me my staff.
Seyton, send out. – Doctor, the thanes fly from me. –

---

35 *moe* more; *skirr* scour   42 *Raze* erase   43 *oblivious antidote* opiate,
medicine of forgetfulness   44 *stuffed* choked up   47 *physic* medicine

Come, sir, dispatch. – If thou couldst, doctor, cast   50
The water of my land, find her disease,
And purge it to a sound and pristine health,
I would applaud thee to the very echo,
That should applaud again. – Pull't off, I say. –
What rhubarb, senna, or what purgative drug
Would scour these English hence? Hear'st thou of them?

DOCTOR
Ay, my good lord. Your royal preparation
Makes us hear something.

MACBETH   Bring it after me!   58
I will not be afraid of death and bane   59
Till Birnam Forest come to Dunsinane.
                            Exeunt [all but the Doctor].

DOCTOR
Were I from Dunsinane away and clear,
Profit again should hardly draw me here.   *[Exit.]*

                            *

Drum and Colors. Enter Malcolm, Siward,   V, iv
Macduff, Siward's Son, Menteith, Caithness,
Angus, [Lennox, Ross,] and Soldiers, marching.

MALCOLM
Cousins, I hope the days are near at hand
That chambers will be safe.   2

MENTEITH   We doubt it nothing.

SIWARD
What wood is this before us?

MENTEITH   The Wood of Birnam.

MALCOLM
Let every soldier hew him down a bough
And bear't before him. Thereby shall we shadow
The numbers of our host and make discovery   6

50 *dispatch* hasten   50–51 *cast . . . water* analyze the urine   58 *it* i.e. the
remainder of the armor   59 *bane* destruction
V, iv Birnam Wood   2 *That chambers* when sleeping-chambers; *nothing*
not at all   6 *discovery* i.e. reports by scouts

Err in report of us.

SOLDIERS   It shall be done.

SIWARD
We learn no other but the confident tyrant
Keeps still in Dunsinane and will endure
Our setting down before't.

MALCOLM   'Tis his main hope,
11   For where there is advantage to be gone
12   Both more and less have given him the revolt,
And none serve with him but constrainèd things
Whose hearts are absent too.

14 MACDUFF   Let our just censures
15   Attend the true event, and put we on
Industrious soldiership.

SIWARD   The time approaches
That will with due decision make us know
What we shall say we have and what we owe.
19   Thoughts speculative their unsure hopes relate,
20   But certain issue strokes must arbitrate –
21   Towards which advance the war.   *Exeunt, marching.*

*

V, v   *Enter Macbeth, Seyton, and Soldiers, with Drum
and Colors.*

MACBETH
Hang out our banners on the outward walls.
2   The cry is still, 'They come!' Our castle's strength
Will laugh a siege to scorn. Here let them lie
Till famine and the ague eat them up.
5   Were they not forced with those that should be ours,
We might have met them dareful, beard to beard,

---

11 *advantage* opportunity   12 *more and less* high and low   14 *just censures*
impartial judgment   15 *Attend* await; *put we on* let us put on   19 *relate*
convey   20 *certain issue* the definite outcome; *arbitrate* decide   21 *war*
army
V, v Within Dunsinane Castle   2 *still* always   5 *forced* reinforced

And beat them backward home.
    A cry within of women.   What is that noise?

SEYTON

It is the cry of women, my good lord.   *[Exit.]*

MACBETH

I have almost forgot the taste of fears.
The time has been my senses would have cooled
To hear a night-shriek, and my fell of hair   11
Would at a dismal treatise rouse and stir   12
As life were in't. I have supped full with horrors.
Direness, familiar to my slaughterous thoughts,   14
Cannot once start me.   15
    [Enter Seyton.] Wherefore was that cry?

SEYTON

The Queen, my lord, is dead.

MACBETH

She should have died hereafter:
There would have been a time for such a word.
To-morrow, and to-morrow, and to-morrow
Creeps in this petty pace from day to day
To the last syllable of recorded time,
And all our yesterdays have lighted fools
The way to dusty death. Out, out, brief candle!
Life's but a walking shadow, a poor player
That struts and frets his hour upon the stage
And then is heard no more. It is a tale
Told by an idiot, full of sound and fury,
Signifying nothing.
    Enter a Messenger.
Thou com'st to use thy tongue: thy story quickly!

MESSENGER

Gracious my lord,
I should report that which I say I saw,   31
But know not how to do't.

---

11 *fell* pelt 12 *treatise* story 14 *Direness* horror 15 *start me* make me
start 31 *say* i.e. affirm

MACBETH   Well, say, sir.
MESSENGER
  As I did stand my watch upon the hill,
  I looked toward Birnam, and anon methought
  The wood began to move.
MACBETH   Liar and slave!
MESSENGER
  Let me endure your wrath if't be not so.
  Within this three mile may you see it coming.
  I say, a moving grove.
MACBETH   If thou speak'st false,
  Upon the next tree shalt thou hang alive
40 Till famine cling thee. If thy speech be sooth,
  I care not if thou dost for me as much.
42 I pull in resolution, and begin
43 To doubt th' equivocation of the fiend,
  That lies like truth. 'Fear not, till Birnam Wood
  Do come to Dunsinane!' and now a wood
  Comes toward Dunsinane. Arm, arm, and out!
47 If this which he avouches does appear,
  There is nor flying hence nor tarrying here.
  I 'gin to be aweary of the sun,
  And wish th' estate o' th' world were now undone.
  Ring the alarum bell! Blow wind, come wrack,
52 At least we'll die with harness on our back.   *Exeunt.*

*

V, vi   *Drum and Colors. Enter Malcolm, Siward,*
        Macduff, and their Army, with boughs.
MALCOLM
  Now near enough. Your leavy screens throw down
  And show like those you are. You, worthy uncle,
  Shall with my cousin, your right noble son,

40 *cling* shrivel; *sooth* truth   42 *pull in* curb, check   43 *doubt* suspect;
equivocation double-talk   47 *avouches* affirms   52 *harness* armor
V, vi Fields outside Dunsinane Castle

Lead our first battle. Worthy Macduff and we   4
Shall take upon's what else remains to do,
According to our order.   6
SIWARD   Fare you well.
Do we but find the tyrant's power to-night,   7
Let us be beaten if we cannot fight.
MACDUFF
Make all our trumpets speak, give them all breath,
Those clamorous harbingers of blood and death.

> *Exeunt. Alarums continued.*

*

Enter Macbeth.   V, vii
MACBETH
They have tied me to a stake. I cannot fly,
But bear-like I must fight the course. What's he   2
That was not born of woman ? Such a one
Am I to fear, or none.
> *Enter Young Siward.*

YOUNG SIWARD
What is thy name ?
MACBETH   Thou'lt be afraid to hear it.
YOUNG SIWARD
No, though thou call'st thyself a hotter name
Than any is in hell.
MACBETH   My name 's Macbeth.
YOUNG SIWARD
The devil himself could not pronounce a title
More hateful to mine ear.
MACBETH   No, nor more fearful.
YOUNG SIWARD
Thou liest, abhorrèd tyrant ! With my sword
I'll prove the lie thou speak'st.
> *Fight, and Young Siward slain.*

---

4 *battle* battalion   6 *order* battle-plan   7 *power* forces
V, vii The same   2 *course* attack (like a bear tied to a stake and baited by
dogs or men)

MACBETH   Thou wast born of woman.
But swords I smile at, weapons laugh to scorn,
Brandished by man that's of a woman born.   *Exit.*
     Alarums. Enter Macduff.

MACDUFF
That way the noise is. Tyrant, show thy face !
If thou beest slain and with no stroke of mine,
My wife and children's ghosts will haunt me still.
17   I cannot strike at wretched kerns, whose arms
18   Are hired to bear their staves. Either thou, Macbeth,
Or else my sword with an unbattered edge
20   I sheathe again undeeded. There thou shouldst be :
By this great clatter one of greatest note
22   Seems bruited. Let me find him, Fortune,
And more I beg not !   *Exit. Alarums.*
     Enter Malcolm and Siward.

SIWARD
24   This way, my lord. The castle 's gently rend'red :
The tyrant's people on both sides do fight,
The noble thanes do bravely in the war,
27   The day almost itself professes yours
And little is to do.
MALCOLM   We have met with foes
29   That strike beside us.
SIWARD   Enter, sir, the castle.
                Exeunt. Alarum.

V, viii   *Enter Macbeth.*

MACBETH
Why should I play the Roman fool and die
2   On mine own sword ? Whiles I see lives, the gashes
Do better upon them.
     Enter Macduff.

---

17 *kerns* soldiers of meanest rank   18 *staves* spears   20 *undeeded* not glori-
fied by deeds   22 *bruited* reported   24 *rend'red* surrendered   27 *itself*
professes declares itself   29 *beside us* at our side (?), without trying to hit
us (?)
V, viii   2 *lives* living bodies

MACDUFF   Turn, hellhound, turn!

MACBETH
Of all men else I have avoided thee.
But get thee back! My soul is too much charged   5
With blood of thine already.

MACDUFF   I have no words;
My voice is in my sword, thou bloodier villain
Than terms can give thee out!
        Fight. Alarum.

MACBETH   Thou losest labor.
As easy mayst thou the intrenchant air   9
With thy keen sword impress as make me bleed.   10
Let fall thy blade on vulnerable crests.
I bear a charmèd life, which must not yield
To one of woman born.

MACDUFF   Despair thy charm,   13
And let the angel whom thou still hast served   14
Tell thee, Macduff was from his mother's womb
Untimely ripped.

MACBETH
Accursèd be that tongue that tells me so,
For it hath cowed my better part of man!   18
And be these juggling fiends no more believed,
That palter with us in a double sense,   20
That keep the word of promise to our ear
And break it to our hope. I'll not fight with thee.

MACDUFF
Then yield thee, coward,
And live to be the show and gaze o' th' time.   24
We'll have thee, as our rarer monsters are,   25
Painted upon a pole, and underwrit   26
'Here may you see the tyrant.'

---

5 *charged* burdened   9 *intrenchant* incapable of being trenched (gashed)
10 *impress* leave a mark on   13 *Despair* despair of   14 *angel* i.e. of the host of
Lucifer; *still* always   18 *better part of man* most manly side   20 *palter*
quibble   24 *gaze* sight   25 *monsters* freaks   26 *Painted upon a pole*
pictured on a showman's banner

MACBETH   I will not yield,
To kiss the ground before young Malcolm's feet
And to be baited with the rabble's curse.
Though Birnam Wood be come to Dunsinane,
And thou opposed, being of no woman born,
Yet I will try the last. Before my body
I throw my warlike shield. Lay on, Macduff,
34   And damned be him that first cries 'Hold, enough!'
                          Exeunt fighting. Alarums.
                          [Re-]enter fighting, and Macbeth slain.
                          [Exit Macduff.]

                          *

Retreat and flourish. Enter, with Drum and Colors,
Malcolm, Siward, Ross, Thanes, and Soldiers.

MALCOLM
I would the friends we miss were safe arrived.

SIWARD
36   Some must go off; and yet, by these I see,
So great a day as this is cheaply bought.

MALCOLM
Macduff is missing, and your noble son.

ROSS
Your son, my lord, has paid a soldier's debt.
He only lived but till he was a man,
The which no sooner had his prowess confirmed
42   In the unshrinking station where he fought
But like a man he died.

SIWARD   Then he is dead?

ROSS
Ay, and brought off the field. Your cause of sorrow
Must not be measured by his worth, for then
It hath no end.

---

34 s.d. *Exeunt . . . slain* (after this action the scene apparently shifts to within Dunsinane Castle; cf. V, vii, 29)   **36** *go off* perish; *these* i.e. these here assembled   **42** *unshrinking station* place from which he did not retreat

SIWARD   Had he his hurts before?

ROSS
Ay, on the front.

SIWARD   Why then, God's soldier be he.
Had I as many sons as I have hairs,
I would not wish them to a fairer death:
And so his knell is knolled.

MALCOLM   He's worth more sorrow,
And that I'll spend for him.

SIWARD   He's worth no more.
They say he parted well and paid his score,   52
And so, God be with him. Here comes newer comfort.
Enter Macduff, with Macbeth's head.

MACDUFF
Hail, King, for so thou art. Behold where stands
Th' usurper's cursèd head. The time is free.   55
I see thee compassed with thy kingdom's pearl,   56
That speak my salutation in their minds,
Whose voices I desire aloud with mine –
Hail, King of Scotland!

ALL   Hail, King of Scotland!
Flourish.

MALCOLM
We shall not spend a large expense of time
Before we reckon with your several loves   61
And make us even with you. My Thanes and kinsmen,   62
Henceforth be Earls, the first that ever Scotland
In such an honor named. What's more to do
Which would be planted newly with the time –   65
As calling home our exiled friends abroad
That fled the snares of watchful tyranny,
Producing forth the cruel ministers   68

---

52 *parted* departed; *score* reckoning   55 *free* released from tyranny   56
compassed surrounded   61 *reckon* come to an accounting   62 *make us even
with you* repay you   65 *would be planted newly with the time* i.e. should be
done at the outset of this new era   68 *ministers* agents

Of this dead butcher and his fiend-like queen,
70 Who (as 'tis thought) by self and violent hands
Took off her life – this, and what needful else
That calls upon us, by the grace of Grace
73 We will perform in measure, time, and place.
So thanks to all at once and to each one,
Whom we invite to see us crowned at Scone.

Flourish. Exeunt omnes.

70 *self and violent* her own violent   73 *in measure* with decorum; *time, and place* at the proper time and place

FOR THE BEST IN PAPERBACKS, LOOK FOR THE 🐧

In every corner of the world, on every subject under the sun, Penguin represents quality and variety—the very best in publishing today.

For complete information about books available from Penguin—including Pelicans, Puffins, Peregrines, and Penguin Classics—and how to order them, write to us at the appropriate address below. Please note that for copyright reasons the selection of books varies from country to country.

In the United Kingdom: For a complete list of books available from Penguin in the U.K., please write to *Dept E.P., Penguin Books Ltd, Harmondsworth, Middlesex, UB7 0DA*.

In the United States: For a complete list of books available from Penguin in the U.S., please write to *Dept BA, Penguin, Box 120, Bergenfield, New Jersey 07621-0120*.

In Canada: For a complete list of books available from Penguin in Canada, please write to *Penguin Books Ltd, 2801 John Street, Markham, Ontario L3R 1B4*.

In Australia: For a complete list of books available from Penguin in Australia, please write to the *Marketing Department, Penguin Books Ltd, P.O. Box 257, Ringwood, Victoria 3134*.

In New Zealand: For a complete list of books available from Penguin in New Zealand, please write to the *Marketing Department, Penguin Books (NZ) Ltd, Private Bag, Takapuna, Auckland 9*.

In India: For a complete list of books available from Penguin, please write to *Penguin Overseas Ltd, 706 Eros Apartments, 56 Nehru Place, New Delhi, 110019*.

In Holland: For a complete list of books available from Penguin in Holland, please write to *Penguin Books Nederland B.V., Postbus 195, NL-1380AD Weesp, Netherlands*.

In Germany: For a complete list of books available from Penguin, please write to *Penguin Books Ltd, Friedrichstrasse 10-12, D-6000 Frankfurt Main 1, Federal Republic of Germany*.

In Spain: For a complete list of books available from Penguin in Spain, please write to *Longman, Penguin España, Calle San Nicolas 15, E-28013 Madrid, Spain*.

In Japan: For a complete list of books available from Penguin in Japan, please write to *Longman Penguin Japan Co Ltd, Yamaguchi Building, 2-12-9 Kanda Jimbocho, Chiyoda-Ku, Tokyo 101, Japan*.

The Pelican Shakespeare

_____ 0-14-071430-8	**All's Well That Ends Well** Barish (ed.)	2.95
_____ 0-14-071420-0	**Antony and Cleopatra** Mack (ed.)	3.50
_____ 0-14-071417-0	**As You Like It** Sargent (ed.)	2.95
_____ 0-14-071432-4	**The Comedy of Errors** Jorgensen (ed.)	3.50
_____ 0-14-071402-2	**Coriolanus** Levin (ed.)	3.50
_____ 0-14-071428-6	**Cymbeline** Heilman (ed.)	3.95
_____ 0-14-071405-7	**Hamlet** Farnham (ed.)	2.50
_____ 0-14-071407-3	**Henry IV, Part I** Shaaber (ed.)	2.50
_____ 0-14-071408-1	**Henry IV, Part II** Chester (ed.)	3.50
_____ 0-14-071409-X	**Henry V** Harbage (ed.)	3.50
_____ 0-14-071434-0	**Henry VI (Revised Edition), Part I** Bevington (ed.)	2.95
_____ 0-14-071435-9	**Henry VI (Revised Edition), Parts II and III** Bevington (ed.) Turner (ed.)	3.50
_____ 0-14-071436-7	**Henry VIII** Hoeniger (ed.)	2.95
_____ 0-14-071422-7	**Julius Caesar** Johnson (ed.)	2.95
_____ 0-14-071426-X	**King John** Ribner (ed.)	3.50
_____ 0-14-071414-6	**King Lear** Harbage (ed.)	2.95
_____ 0-14-071427-8	**Love's Labor's Lost** Harbage (ed.)	3.50
_____ 0-14-071401-4	**Macbeth** Harbage (ed.)	2.95
_____ 0-14-071403-0	**Measure for Measure** Bald (ed.)	2.95
_____ 0-14-071421-9	**The Merchant of Venice** Stirling (ed.)	2.95
_____ 0-14-071424-3	**The Merry Wives of Windsor** Bowers (ed.)	3.50

_____	0-14-071418-9	**A Midsummer Night's Dream** Doral (ed.)	2.95
_____	0-14-071412-X	**Much Ado About Nothing** Bennett (ed.)	3.50
_____	0-14-071437-5	**The Narrative Poems** Shakespeare	3.95
_____	0-14-071410-3	**Othello** Bentley (ed.)	3.50
_____	0-14-071438-3	**Pericles** McManaway (ed.)	3.50
_____	0-14-071406-5	**Richard II** Black (ed.)	3.50
_____	0-14-071416-2	**Richard III** Evans (ed.)	3.50
_____	0-14-071419-7	**Romeo and Juliet** Hankins (ed.)	2.75
_____	0-14-071423-5	**Sonnets** Shakespeare	2.95
_____	0-14-071425-1	**The Taming of the Shrew** Hosley (ed.)	2.95
_____	0-14-071415-4	**The Tempest** Frye (ed.)	2.25
_____	0-14-071429-4	**Timon of Athens** Hinman (ed.)	2.95
_____	0-14-071433-2	**Titus Andronicus** Cross (ed.)	3.50
_____	0-14-071413-8	**Troilus and Cressida** Whitaker (ed.)	3.50
_____	0-14-071411-1	**Twelfth Night** Prouty (ed.)	2.95
_____	0-14-071431-6	**The Two Gentlemen of Verona (Revised Edition)** Jackson (ed.)	3.50
_____	0-14-071404-9	**The Winter's Tale** Maxwell (ed.)	2.95

The Penguin Shakespeare

_____	0-14-070720-4	**All's Well That Ends Well** Everett (ed.)	3.75
_____	0-14-070731-X	**Antony and Cleopatra** Jones (ed.)	3.75
_____	0-14-070714-X	**As You Like It** Oliver (ed.)	3.75
_____	0-14-070725-5	**The Comedy of Errors** Wells (ed.)	3.75
_____	0-14-070703-4	**Coriolanus** Hibbard (ed.)	3.75
_____	0-14-070734-4	**Hamlet** Spencer (ed.)	3.75
_____	0-14-070718-2	**Henry IV, Part I** Davison (ed.)	3.75
_____	0-14-070728-X	**Henry IV, Part II** Davison (ed.)	3.75
_____	0-14-070708-5	**Henry V** Humphreys (ed.)	3.75
_____	0-14-070735-2	**Henry VI, Part I** Sanders (ed.)	3.75
_____	0-14-070736-0	**Henry VI, Part II** Sanders (ed.)	3.75
_____	0-14-070737-9	**Henry VI, Part III** Sanders (ed.)	3.75
_____	0-14-070722-0	**Henry VIII** Humphreys (ed.)	3.75
_____	0-14-070704-2	**Julius Caesar** Sanders (ed.)	3.75

FOR THE BEST IN PAPERBACKS, LOOK FOR THE 🐧

FOR THE BEST DRAMA, LOOK FOR THE